JONATHAN ASHLEY is the author of *Out of Mercy* and *The Cost of Doing Business*. His work has appeared in *Crime Factory, A Twist of Noir, LEO Weekly, Kentucky Magazine* and *Yellow Mama*.

THE COST OF DOING BUSINESS

JONATHAN ASHLEY

280 STEPS

1

PEOPLE WHO SAY guilt is a wasted emotion have obviously never met a true sociopath.

I have.

I met dozens of them over the last three years, ever since I decided to turn my used bookstore into a front for the biggest heroin operation Louisville had ever seen. I didn't intend to become a drug dealer, to hurt people, to murder fellow human beings and bury them in the woods of LaGrange, sink them in the Ohio with cinder blocks chained to their ankles, or let them rapidly decompose, covered with lye in an abandoned farmhouse I bought after making my first million.

My intention, what led to all of this, was to get a speed freak out of my life for good. I had my own problems, dope and alcohol, and desired to save both a romantic relationship and my business, Twice Told Books. But as with so much that followed, washing my hands of a drug fiend who depended on me for his fix turned out to be much messier than I could have ever predicted.

Louisville only has two times a year in which the city, almost overnight, becomes worth living. If one arrives in Spring or Fall, the tourist or native will find perfect weather, sunsets sinking into the Ohio River buttressed by skyscrapers, ancient bridges with steamboats chugging along underneath. If you travel south of the river, toward my neighborhood, you might pass a few undesirable avenues, those that run through Smoketown most likely, where black and white children in hand-me-down underclothes block the middle of the street playing with hula hoops and deflated soccer balls, avoiding whatever horrors their parents perpetuate in the shotgun shacks on either side of the blacktop. However, the trip through the slums won't last long, and when a tourist or out-of-towner reaches the Highlands, without fail they're treated to the best of New York City Bohemia packed into a two mile strip of Bardstown Road. One might almost reach sensory overload as the Highlands surrounds them; the tattoo parlors, the coffee shops, and record stores, not to mention greasy spoons, ethnic joints and five star restaurants alike. Then there are the neighborhood's residents, mostly transplants from the impoverished south end, the affluent east, and cities as far away as Los Angeles.

Louisville had become a city of enterprise, criminal and otherwise. Our population had grown by thirty percent in the last six years. Our music scene had begun to rival that of Austin. Just two weeks before my ascension from part-time middle-man to aspiring dope kingpin, I'd gotten to watch Catherine Livingston play right in my own bookstore, the last of the independents left in Louisville. Paul, my part-time manager, and an aging punk rocker, supplemented the income from disability, financial aid from working on his Master's, and the cash I paid him at the store with pot deals. He also made a little on the side from the monthly sale of his Adderall prescription, and session work as a drummer. The guy was an encyclopedia. He could tell you who played saxophone on track five of Merle Haggard's thirty-fifth, out-of-print duets album guest starring Willie, Waylon, and, as Paul called the least famous troubadour, "The Ever-Tragic Tompall Glaser." He could also recite in detail and at great length the sexual fetishes of all the classic authors, from James Joyce to Frank O'Connor. We sat upstairs and watched Catherine through loosely drawn blinds, contemplating, as most men in the crowd likely were, *her* possible fetishes. Catherine, with her beehive hairdo and real-woman curves seemed the closest figurehead I'd ever know comparable to Dylan's Little Richard; the Kentucky beauty may as well have been from the moon. Her values and worldview matched something akin to a drifter or even an Outlaw from the great depression. She cared only about the way she treated others, the needs of the day, and the greater purpose of making the world a slightly better place. Anything else she'd openly regard as cheap and beneath her attention and worry.

"You look like I feel." Paul sat behind my desk and leaned back in my father's creaking swivel chair.

"So do several venereal diseases," I came back quickly. "We could be here all night if we started assembling those kind of lists though, so let's change subjects. For once let's talk about something light, positive even."

Paul always crossed his legs as he rested his feet on the wide oak top of my desk. We were silent for a few minutes. As usual, neither of us could think of anything nice to say.

"Long week," Paul said.

"Long week?" I sat on the wicker-back chair against the wall to Paul's left, my head turned south toward the window and Catherine beyond. "Long week, Paul?" I repeated his words again. "Long days, long week, and a long shitty life, you ask me." My eyes wouldn't leave Catherine. I watched her through the half-drawn blinds, mouthing her lyrics which I'd grown up singing. We knew each other. She probably would have described me, at this point, as a friend. But the first impression I made at a late night barbecue would've ruined my chances with any woman, no matter what sexual prowess I might have possessed. The night she learned my name, two bartenders had thrown me out of Nach, the latest, poshest joint in town. I despised their clientele with such absurd intensity, such pathological disdain that late at night when sleep was away on business, I'd lay in the dark imagining what the trendy little bar might look like in flames, the doors nailed shut, the patrons stuck inside—this part of the fantasy had never been worked out in any detail. The particulars didn't matter, and leaving one or two parts of the fire plan for later scrutiny did not fail to pause or put off the womanly screams of bearded, backbone-lacking twenty-somethings in my fantasy as I watched the whole row house collapse in flames on repeat in my mind.

While she knew nothing of my fire and death fantasies, Catherine still did not have the greatest first impression of yours truly. In fact, she witnessed me falling off the bar's balcony out back from where she sang, landing on a bar employee tending a grill and ruining the dozens of tofu steaks. Catherine stopped her set and ran down the balcony stairs with her guitar at her side. She was the first to attend to me, to see if the incorrigible party crasher had done any real damage to himself. We'd remained friendly ever since. That night, at Nach, before I picked two fights and the staff finally banned me indefinitely, Catherine introduced me to the recent bane of my existence, Irina. Lately, I'd felt a mixture of gratitude and disdain for having ever met the roan-haired manic depressive. I'd table the Thank You letter to Catherine until we saw how things played out, whether Irina would finally break my heart for good, or if she'd just come back again.

"She just needs time," Catherine had told me as Paul and I helped her set up on the small stage Paul had built just for the show.

"How long you think we're talking?" I asked back. "Because I'm aging here."

For her performance, Catherine had let her hair down, raven curls drawing together over her face like a curtain. She'd neglected to attend to the top two snap buttons of her denim shirt, exposing the peaks of her voluminous bust framed by black lace from a bra the size of which I could only speculate and fantasize. I felt guilty, only momentarily, for lusting after Irina's best friend. Then I considered some of the less considerate things Irina had said to me over the past month, and all the guilt dissolved like Catherine's throaty twang into the smoky evening ether.

"You're the human version of those movies they call 'feel good Summer hits'." Paul guffawed. Still laughing, he inquired about my tempestuous love life. "You were

hitting a different coed every weekend then like that..."
the ancient punker snapped his fingers. "Irina fell for you
and from then on, you only had eyes for the innocent
Catholic girl from St. Matthews." Paul threw his hands
in the air, amazed. "Misunderstood Genius. Women
love that shit."

I accepted the half-smoked joint that Paul had bogarted
for the past five minutes. Before he could distract me
or rush my toke, I took two consecutive hits, both long
and smooth, the smoke hitting all the right places. "I
think Irina's done with me. Goddamn, I'm gonna miss
those legs." Handing Paul back his joint, I added, "You'll
be seeing a lot more of me."

"Oh, no." Paul removed his spectacles and asked,
"She gone?"

"Enough," Taking a swig of the Heineken bottle he'd
served himself from the cooler beneath my desk that,
like anyone without an addictive personality, he'd been
nursing reasonably for fifteen minutes. The bottle still
contained a considerable amount of lager when he offered
it. I killed the beer. Paul reached under the desk and
came out with two more sweaty green-tinted bottles.
He accepted my empty one and dropped it in the trash
next to him while I popped the fresher Heineken open
with my lighter, downing half the beer before Paul had
finished opening his own.

"Jesus, kid." Paul stubbed the roach out in the green
ceramic ashtray at the edge of my desk. "Don't look like
you're taking it too well."

"She thinks I'm too morbid. Too negative. She started
referring to me regularly as 'anti-social.'"

"Look up 'malcontent.'" Paul nodded to the massive Webster's dictionary from the late 1960s that lay open, displayed on the leaning podium that stood across the dark office from the windows.

"Am I going to find a picture of me?"

"No, Just an accurate description of your morose ass."

"Don't teach Irina the word."

A knock sounded on the door to my office. Paul and I shared a disconcerted glance, knowing who it'd be, who we'd been expecting since ten p.m.

"Give us a moment and we'll be right there," I shouted over the music, but not loud enough to interrupt the acoustic set below.

The man waiting to enter was Carter Homer Parrant, the most irritating speed freak in three zip codes. He used to work at the bookstore until the weekend he overheard me talking to my on-again/off-again lover, Irina, about the pharmacy's failure to refill her Adderall prescription due to some bureaucratic glitch. Irina called later that day to explain that Carter had dialed her ten times and texted her twenty, making all kinds of absurd promises to get her to hand over the bulk of her pills: "I swear to God on Monday I'll have two hundred bucks for you and the things go for only three a piece on the street... Please, I'll get my parents to loan Jon enough to build five more bookcases and fill them to the brim with first editions."

I slapped the little bastard around for about ten minutes, fired him, and explained that if he ever bothered my woman again I'd hurt him in a place essential to producing a Carter the Second.

"I can't believe I'm going along with this." Paul stood, lifted the biker jacket draped over my desk chair, and headed toward the office restroom. "Shit. After all the annoyance that troglodyte caused you, I can't believe you'd deal with him again." Paul spoke loud enough for Carter to hear outside. In fact, had Catherine not been crowing a hair-raising bridge to her song about Muhammad Ali, the whole store would've been privy to Paul's disdain for the trust fund recipient standing outside my office.

"Calm down." Dealing with Carter in any manner wasn't my idea of a fun Saturday either, but Paul got his Adderall script the second of every month, one day after Carter's monthly check posted. And since Paul desperately needed funds for child support, I felt it prudent to find the quickest and most reliable buyer. Every month Paul allowed me to utilize my long cultivated drug connections to make him a few extra hundred dollars off the ninety round and pink thirty-milligram speed pills.

"Just wait in the goddamn bathroom, okay?" I whispered, heading toward the locked and bolted office door.

"I have to hide because of a speed freak halfwit you're dealing with out of sheer sloth?"

"You're the one who said you needed money." Carter began knocking again as I turned the key, glared at Paul then nodded toward the bathroom. "And you're the one who refuses to stand in the same room with him. So, since I'm such a good friend, I'll do so for you."

The bathroom door behind me closed in sync with the office lamps brightening the hallway as I opened the office door, revealing the emaciated Carter with his Louisville Cardinals ball cap worn cockeyed, his slouching khaki shorts and dirty sandals. Laying eyes on the slump-shouldered urban enthusiast who'd watched *8 Mile* one too many times, the arbitrary nature of fate sideswiped me for a moment. While many may label me an ego-maniac with a severe inferiority complex, I don't advertise my intellect much. However, Forrest Gump could give Carter a run for his money in any competition of wit. Carter's character also left more than a little to be desired. He'd laughingly and openly admitted to ordering his teenage girlfriend to perform fellatio on a cocaine dealer in exchange for two free eight-balls. "Bitch'll do anything I tell her," he'd chortled. "Anything."

Irina, for almost two years now, had been the light of my loins and fire of my life as I called her, a bad riff off the first lines of the book we'd read to one another the first month of our coupling, before and after hours of shameless and enlightening coitus. I'd love to take credit for the humorous play on *Lolita's* widely quoted opening sentence, but the simple truth is that the heroin my favorite dealer Shorty had sold me that afternoon had been uncut china white, the best dope south of Cincinnati in my experienced estimate, and it had left me so cross-eyed with euphoria I'd mixed up the wording.

Carter either lacked foresight and an even moderately healthy level of self-preservation or he purposely disregarded how I felt about the woman; when she called that day and explained how the speed freak had dialed and texted her three times an hour that evening, offering everything but his own phallus for some of her pills. I considered just firing him. Then Irina told me about how she'd told Carter "no" over and over again. She finally reminded my then soon-to-be former employee that her mother had pneumonia and it would be much appreciated if Carter stopped keeping the phone line tied up. Carter then, displaying a level of inconsiderateness rare for even a drug addict, insinuated smugly deception on Irina's part. Carter said, "I-r-i-n-a. You have an iPhone and I think those come with caller ID. Nice try though."

I felt it prudent to escalate things with Carter since he had so blatantly disregarded my overprotective, almost fatherly sentiments regarding Irina—I'd more than once warned him to leave her be after handing over speed I'd acquired for the ingrate. "Irina never knows about any of this if for no other reason than her own recovery." Irina was a member of AA, and had fought a severe substance abuse problem for a decade and had only recently achieved six months clean time.

Carter, simply by exposing Irina to his desperate, junkie behavior, had put her own sobriety at risk. Her abstinence had both saved and strained our relationship as she'd threatened to leave several times. She even cut off contact completely for whole weeks whenever she suspected me of using, a suspicion well founded. Excluding two thirty day stints of clean time, my pathetic best attempts at kicking, I hadn't been completely clean and sober in over five years. And whenever I did kick, I drank like a fish, hiding bottles around the bookstore to nip on so I could get through the day like a good alcoholic.

Lately, I'd sent up no red flags, no indicators that might reveal the habit I'd been hiding. I'm grateful that it was during one of those brief stints of sobriety that I first got to kiss her, us both stumbling like drunks on the sidewalk in front of my store after a candle-lit Italian dinner at a bistro up the strip called Le Gallo Rosa where they'd sectioned off a corner upstairs just for us. The owners and management treated me like black market royalty as the kitchen and wait staff had done with Ray Liotta in *GoodFellas*. Irina shoved me against the glass storefront of the clothing boutique next door to my shop. I dropped the keys with which I'd been fumbling to get into the store so I could seduce her when she beat me to the punch, almost angrily pushing her lips against mine and squeezing my cheeks with both hands as if I might try to escape.

Perhaps the memory of that night and so many like it that followed saved Carter's life for a while, since Irina and the joyous days she'd granted me were still lingering in my mind when I'd arrived at Carter's. When Carter opened the front door after I'd knocked loudly and repetitively, I delivered an open-hand slap so hard that he fell from his stoop into the bushes, telling him he was fired as he rubbed the pain from the side of his face and I headed across the street where I'd parked my Alero.

Tonight, the last thing I would've guessed, while Catherine sang her hard luck ballads below us and I placed the prescription bottle Carter intended to buy on the desk, was for Irina to call right as Carter counted out the money for his pills. Irina explained that Carter had not only turned to harassing her again, but that he offered for her remaining Addies, not just a ridiculous amount of his parent's money, but the phone number to the best cocaine connection he'd ever come across. "He also told me he'd buy me an eight ball," She was crying. "I feel like I'm gonna throw up, Jon. What's wrong with him? He's a fiend. Does he fucking know what hearing that shit does to me?"

"I'll take care of it." I slowly closed my eyes and shook my head dejectedly. The night had just taken a sharp turn for the worst, at least for Carter.

"Don't do anything rash..." She drew in a deep, dramatic breath. "Jesus. I shouldn't have called you. I know how you can get about this kind of stuff. Just don't do something stupid. I know how..."

"You know how I am about people I love?" With the phone lodged between my shoulder and ear I drew the blinds to the window looking down on the crowd of Catherine Livingston fans, waiting for her band who'd just joined her on stage for the second half of her set to tune up and kick off the next number.

Irina said, "Yeah, I know how you are about that kind of thing. I heard about all the bar fights and..."

I hung up as she continued her protest. I would've stayed on the line longer but the lady doth protested too goddamn much and I had an immediate need for strict and brutal retribution. Little Carter cakes would suffer the worst fate a junkie could imagine for his transgression.

"No Addies." Looking at him only once after my

declaration, a smile cracked the lower half of my face, a perfect break in my permanent scowl. My momentary mirth stood in harsh contrast to the thinning front line of hair and the deep furrows etched in my brow from too many years of too much failure and regret.

The kid looked like someone had just told him his parents had been shotgunned, Capote-style, blood all over their snoopy pajamas in the basement of his childhood home. He had the look of a expectant junkie discovering his dealer short, or in my case, unwilling.

"Wha-at?" He broke the syllable in half as he laughed dramatically. "You're fucking with me, right?"

I shook my head "no" as I lightly put down my cell, and took a seat behind my desk overflowing with books and bills. The brat would undoubtedly throw a fit as all of his kind do when denied their desires.

2

"LISTEN." CARTER PLACED his palms together, a wretch's prayer to no one in particular, to anyone who would help him. "I don't know what's changed, why you're being this way..."

"Please." I held up my own two hands, forming a stop-motion gesture. "Just stop, Carter. Stop the whole damned half-retarded, dog and pony show that works on your family and little junkie girlfriends. You're trying to bullshit a far more renowned bullshitter and it ain't gonna work. You called Irina again. You're cut off. It's that simple."

"You motherfucker." Carter huffed and puffed and if he could have, he would've blown my business straight to hell, but the breath he let out was stifled by too many sleepless nights and two packs of cigarettes a day. "At least tell me why." Carter fell into Paul's favorite armchair of worn and torn black leather. One time, Paul pulled Carter out of the same chair by the little punk's brightly red-dyed hair, and said, "You sit in my place again, I'll run you through with a broad sword, peasant." Paul loved speaking as if we lived in thirteenth-century Europe. He saw us as noble rogues, rascals who filled each waking moment with drink and plans to cornhole the closest Lord's fair lady. Sadly, our lives were far less filled with meaning or adventure, just nights plagued with characters like the one sitting across from me, the dejected junkie who had gone too far, the desperate loser who would sell me and Paul out to the Louisville Metro Police for enough to buy a quarter gram of heroin or half an eight ball.

"You ever ask yourself, Carter..." I stared fixedly at the bathroom door, pondering when to call for Paul. I decided to force Carter to face a real question that involved his own mortality and behavior patterns, a question he'd no doubt shirk unless answering brought him closer to his high. "You ever ask yourself, 'Why don't I have any real friends?'" The cigarette I'd been playing with, rolling from finger to finger, began to weigh heavily as I grasped the Marlboro in my palm. My head and heart were both weighed down, for I knew the ordeal of ejecting Carter from my office and store had only just begun and the little shit would drag it out as long as he could, making sure, if he didn't get his fix, that I'd feel as much of his pain as he could disperse. "You ever notice the only people you speak to are other druggies and smack dealers? You ever get tired of having to beg your parents for money and make up excuses for why you've plowed through your trust fund check by the end of the month's first week?"

"What the hell does any of that shit have to do with me getting my Addies?" Carter pushed the chair a few feet back with his big ass as he indignantly rose like a long, half-dead bastard child of a Phoenix. "I'm sorry you're having problems with Irina."

"You got a lot of nerve, kid." I considered standing and knocking loudly on the bathroom door for Paul's assistance, or perhaps even just yelling for my closest partner in crime to come out and join Carter's pity party. The fiend obviously needed more attendees for his Oscar-worthy performance that rivaled Jodi Foster's weeping rape victim in *The Accused*. I chortled and stood, pressing my palms deeply into my desktop. "Someday, somehow, kid," I stepped calmly, slowly toward the locked bathroom door, behind which Paul no doubt giggled and fumed at the absurd mania he'd been forced to listen to in miserable silence, "you're gonna be forced to stop lying to yourself, at least for long enough for the truth to paralyze you. I hope you're somewhere safe when that happens."

"You deserve a whore like Irina to run your life for you." Carter stared numbly out the half-blinded window as the drummer clicked off the first song with a full band backing the torch singer, each word audible sex appeal, her voice worn velvet sandpaper. She deserved a better audience than me and Carter. Neither of us were listening anyway. He searched the recesses of his mind, those few brain cells left free from the ruin of meth or other dope or the jones his habit constantly left him fighting.

"Come on out." I said lowly, tapping the rusted knob of the bathroom door lightly with my knuckle.

"You sure?" Paul laughed his words while Carter turned. His eyes met mine and something paranoid and primitive flashed across his bloodshot whites. He'd probably taken Xanax or perhaps even one of his mother's pain pills to help with his comedown, but I only had a moment to meditate on the kid's pharmacological practices. He took two quick steps toward me. His words came out slow and slurred as his mind reverted to the caveman's default setting of fight or flight.

"Who the hell's in there?" Carter was gone. The mix of anger over losing one of his best speed connects and hopelessness at the thought of another sleepless night of abject depression had combined, rendering him infantile and, as anyone who'd dealt with a desperate tweeker, prone to delusion.

"Calm down." I knocked again and yelled for Paul to come out, addressing my long-time roadie by his first name, hopefully causing something akin to logic to click in Carter's sick brain. The bolt and knob locks unhatched on the other side of the bathroom door. Carter stared as if beyond the entrance to the latrine awaited every dope dealer that had ever shorted him or sold him fake shit.

"You trying to jam me up, Jon Boy?" Carter yelled and moved a few paces closer to me. Carter and I had never liked one another. It started when we were kids and only grew worse in our twenties. Since the first time we saw each other after high school graduation, a deep grudge had grown. I unknowingly tried to seduce his petite little blond girlfriend at Cahoots, one of the worst dives in Louisville, the dirtiest dope bar on the Bardstown strip. Her name was Tiffany or Brittany or one of those awful valley girl designations born into popularity during the 1980s when parents began becoming their kid's best friends rather than, as had been practiced in most cultures throughout history, examples of humanity. Brit or Tiff happened to be one in a long line of successive gold diggers who preyed on Carter's weaknesses and misconceptions until they realized his parents only gave him enough money each month to reach the periphery of utter self-destruction. Then, like women whose attachments with a man all hinged on finance, they left when the well's water ceased to rise at a rate that met their satisfaction.

"Jon Boy?" Paul entered the room as I stood aside with the door open. He removed his leather waistcoat, treating our unwelcome guest to a candid shot of his wide and well sculpted biceps, forearms like Louisville Sluggers, and hands as large and worn as ancient sledgehammer heads. Paul had always been overly self-conscious about how he looked, and worked out every day to avoid developing a middle-age beer gut. "I didn't know little Car-Car had a pet name for you, Jon." Paul lit a Marlboro with the dying ember of his last, flicking the smoldering stub against Carter's chest. Carter flailed like a nearly dead victim of Alien impregnation, brushing wildly at his sweatshirt to be sure he'd rid his person of the lit cigarette and whatever remained of the cherry. I stepped closer to Carter, spotting the still-lit cigarette burning a tiny hole in the red and beige Oriental Rug my father had left me from his travels in China when he worked for one of the largest oil companies on the globe as a PR man. As I leaned down to retrieve the offending Marlboro, Paul's giggling ceased.

Carter's conjoined clenched fists came down, making harsh contact with the base of my neck, knocking me flat on my face, the cigarette stubbed out in a fashion I'd never had chosen, smashed between my chest and the old man's rug, one of the only things my lush father hadn't squandered or drank up.

"Son of a bitch." Paul yelled somewhere above me, his words growing louder as the heels of his Doc Martens combat boots stomped determinedly toward where I lay, where Carter hovered above me. It took me what seemed like a full minute to simply move my head, to shift cheeks and rest my right side on the carpet in long need of a vacuuming. The delay was probably due to the shock of the prior moments' cataclysmal, near miraculous event, Carter piecing together the salt flakes that made up his spinal column for long enough to engage in such an uncharacteristically masculine and, frankly, brave action; the coward had struck me. As I pulled focus on my assailant, only the faint dimpled ghost of Carter's sneer remained. Paul entered my frame of vision from the left, his fist following close behind, soaring past his face, obscuring his beet red cheeks and flaring nostrils only briefly before connecting with Carter's jaw.

As the harsh snapping sound, indubitably the severance of some conjoining functionary bone in Carter's lower skull, continued to echo Carter fell not two feet from where I lay, cupping his wounded jaw and mouth with his palms. His scream, only stifled momentarily by whatever Paul had broken, seemed sufficiently muffled by the chorus Cathy sang below us, the pedal steel and snare drum deafening all noise save the immediate. I pushed myself up from the carpet and stood between Carter and Paul. Carter had rose to his knees, still rubbing his jaw. It was my turn to get a shot at the little savage.

But Carter surprised me again.

While I caught my breath, struggling to stay on my feet, Carter came up from the floor with a quickness by all laws of reason impossible. The depleted son of a bitch should not have possessed such speed. His pupils shot left then right, pausing at the sight of the wet bar near the window, caddy corner to my desk. In keeping with Carter's affinity for the obvious, he grabbed a half-empty bottle of Jack Daniels by the neck and raised it over the bar top. I should have known what was coming, but not until he broke the glass and the contents splattered against the blinded window did I realize he'd decided to mimic the first move of any novice in a B-movie bar fight.

"Thought that was pretty fucking funny." He forced a bloody sneer. The tip of his upper lip had swelled out. The lump Paul created with the haymaker that had knocked Carter on his ass had already grown to the size of a small grape. "You two assholes thought fucking with me was funny." Carter aimed the jagged end of the broken bottle, taking turns pointing his makeshift weapon at me then Paul.

"I still think you're funny." Paul shrugged. "If I didn't find humor in your pathetic attempt at a life, I might just waste my energy hating you."

"Which has been my big pitfall." I eyed the dictionary on the podium, less than a foot to my left. I gauged the distance between me and Carter, roughly the width of the room, then considered the three feet I'd have to sprint to get my hands on the Webster's. Before I could over think my move, I lunged toward the podium, placed all ten fingers around the open dictionary. Carter leaped, raising the broken bottle with its sharp open bottom extending from his clenched fist like a serial killer's butcher knife in some slasher flick.

I didn't have time to think. The kid was almost on me, a hair more than arm's length. I didn't have time to even lift the massive book or ascertain an unguarded weak spot where I could knock the wind out of him.

"Fuck it," I said, too quietly for Carter to hear, and flung the dictionary like one of those Olympic discs. Still high and a bit tight from the booze that I'd poured from the bottle with which Carter had wanted to disfigure me, I actually giggled as the hardback left my hands, imagining me in short shorts and an undershirt, spinning a half dozen times to hike the momentum before tossing the massive reference book, Carter tied up at the end of the athletic field, gagged, praying for the wind to pick up substantially and for the dictionary to miss. I threw the book at him, so to speak, but my smile disappeared as I helplessly watched what followed.

The book stayed closed for the entirety of its flight and hit the demented drug addict in his forearm, forcing his hand back toward his neck, the broken bottle lodging in his windpipe. The book fell, landing open, pages down, on the carpet. A few droplets of blood stained the dust jacket, two shades of red mingling. Carter's arms dangled limply at his side. The bottle's neck pointed at me like a gun barrel. Its broken base remained stuck firmly in Carter's jugular. Every article of clothing had already been stained crimson from what must have been a nicked artery. There was so much blood, the bottle itself began to fill, the dark red fluid pouring like wine from the mouth.

As if waiting for Carter to gain a second wind, Paul and I stood silently until the kid finally collapsed, first to his knees, then on his side, before we slowly, with the most timid baby steps, approached the corpse.

"Why did you do that?" Paul got that wild eyed look that usually betrayed madness, only this time, something new showed in the darker shades of his cold gray irises, a haunting hybrid of loss and panic, although what Paul had lost, at the moment, I couldn't fathom, considering I'd been the one to kill the prick. Later, it became clear that Paul, the smarter partner in crime, at that very instance, standing just outside the coagulating circle of bodily fluids spreading and surrounding the body, knew that our joyful, carefree days filled only with concerns over beer and bill money, had just ended. "Why?" he asked again, as if I'd done this on purpose.

I opened my mouth and closed it several times in slow succession, unable to think of anything appropriate to say. I told myself, staring into Carter's dilating pupils, his face as white as Alaskan snows, that I'd only allow myself a few seconds of grief, guilt, and self-pity. After all, I had a mess to clean up, and the freedom of two blithe degenerates to preserve

3

—

IF YOU WANT revenge, dig two graves. I wound up digging over a dozen. It didn't help. I'd learn that before I finally fled Louisville.

"I can't believe you're just skipping over the murder." Paul hadn't stopped bitching since I'd begun rolling Carter up in the Chinese carpet. "You just killed somebody and you haven't batted an eye."

"Why couldn't he have died closer to the bathroom?" I sighed over-dramatically, the first feigning of emotion I'd attempted since my least favorite doper's violent end.

"Jon…" Paul had been sitting behind my desk, staring vacantly at the office door, which I'd locked after my half-minute grieving process. "You just murdered a man."

I tucked Carter as snugly as I could into the carpet. I'd placed the dictionary, the murder weapon, on his chest, in his clasped hands. I secured the carpet roll with duct tape, but much to my chagrin, and due to my almost reverent refusal to touch the body more than I had to, the head still peeked out from the top hole. "Goddamnit."

"What?" Paul ran his hands through his hair, black and shiny with enough sweat to keep the thick strands patted down like a defeated ducktail. Pit stains the width of frisbees extended from beneath the short sleeves of his blank black tee. "Are you finally grasping the gravity of what's happened here?"

"We most certainly do have a bit of a situation." I sat on the floor a few feet from Carter's stubborn cranium and, supporting my back against the northern office wall, began to press down on the crown of the dead body with my boot heels.

The shades were drawn but I could hear the music lovers on the first floor still tapping feet to the honky tonk bass lines. "Look, Paul." I said, catching my breath. "He's going to be dead a long time so I'd get used to it if I were you."

The crowd went bonkers as Catherine Livingston, Louisville's favorite country crooner, brought her song to a close. It had become chic for anyone, from Long Island princesses to Boston Jews, to wear cowboy boots and western shirts. Maybe it was the proverbial blood on my hands, but my patience for the fatally hip, for my nauseatingly meaningless generation, had substantially decreased since my first murder ten minutes prior. These weren't true rebels at heart lacking causes or even the meandering hippies from whom my parents stole their emasculated philosophies. These people below me and Paul were the painfully predictable who stood for nothing.

At the moment, I not only stood for something, I stood on something—I had my foot on Carter's head, shoving with all my might, hoping to force him further down into the roll of carpet when Paul finally rose and crossed the room, stopping just short of the partially concealed dead man.

"What is wrong with you?" Paul breathed heavily between each slowly pronounced syllable.

"Well, I'm not exactly getting a lot of help here, am I?" I stopped what I was doing to glare up at my friend who, I just began to realize, had remained perhaps too sober for such a grim endeavor. I'd snorted two thirty-milligram Oxycontins before the music had started, before I liberally added booze. Alcohol and opiates were a dangerous mixture of which I'd partaken far too much lately. Had I not had a surprisingly selfless junkie mentor, Jimmy O'Hearn, who currently resided on wing D of LaGrange State Reformatory thirty miles south, I may have remained ignorant of the deadly combination for just long enough to over mix. In other words, at least I knowingly rolled the dice and tried, best I could, to drink more reasonably when I'd been snorting dope.

I tried to explain to Paul how the drugs may have assisted in my current level of moral flexibility.

"Morally flexible?" Paul began pacing as the now dead Carter had right before I'd forever silenced the irritant. Paul's pacing seemed more justified, for his umbrage had to do with life and death, not a speed fix.

"Actually," I took another look at the problem cranium that wouldn't budge then met eyes with Paul again. "He came at me with an extremely sharp object."

"Extremely sharp? It was a broken bottle, not a goddamn machete."

"You're saying he couldn't have murdered me with it?" I let out an obviously forced and farcical laugh, that of a master villain playing devil's advocate with a struggling innocent. "Tell that to his severed trachea."

25

"I'm seriously going to have to reconsider how much time I spend around you."

"You're such a pansy." I stood about an inch from Paul, placed a hand on each shoulder, digging my fingers deep into his muscles as his jaw dropped and he began to draw away at the small smite of my most recent insult.

"So you murder a man in front of me." Paul's voice broke as he slowly pulled closer toward the locked office door. "Then you call me a coward."

"A pansy, actually." I began to lower my voice, getting ready to lay it on him, the emotional blackmail.

I did not want to drag that body to my Alero all by myself.

"I think most people would agree that coward is synonymous with pansy," Paul said.

"Are we really standing over a dead body splitting hairs right now?" I gesticulated wildly. "Are we really doing that? Now the fact of the matter is this. You are an accessory. No. You helped. You punched the bastard."

"That was before I knew you were going to cut his throat."

"Erroneous!" I waved away the notion that I had intentionally slit Carter's jugular. "We both know that first off, it was self-defense since he came at me with a bottle and secondly, I didn't mean to kill him. How was I to know that I had such a great throwing hand? I should've played for the Cincinnati Reds, for Christ's sake."

Paul blinked twice, then a smile slowly began to form and I knew my old loyal friend, full of mischief and criminality, had returned in place of the shocked everyman I'd been dealing with for the last half hour.

"The point is," I began again, "if the police tie this to me and they talk to you within a few days and see your knuckles, you're going to LaGrange with me, brother. We are in this together whether you like it or not. So, in the next little bit we have some very big decisions to make. Do you understand me?"

Paul nodded solemnly.

Once Paul had accepted the inevitability of the rest of the evening, he agreed to go downstairs when Cathy's set had ended and thank the musicians and the crowd and usher everyone out gracefully while I finished cleaning.

Part of the hardwood floor would remain stained until someone spent some money I didn't have replacing the boards. I had to accept that the way Paul had begrudgingly accepted our eventual disposal of Carter's corpse. It didn't matter. I remembered I had another, albeit less valuable, ancient Chinese rug of my father's in the basement that would cover the stain. No one would notice the difference unless for some reason the police raided my house while Paul and I were headed downtown. And as far as I knew, we were so far the only ones who no longer counted Carter among the living.

"They're gone." Paul slammed the door behind him.

"Watch the noise." I rose from behind the roll of carpet where the once annoying Carter now lay silent, void of amphetamines forever. I'd doubled down on the tape. The last thing I wanted was to have to repackage Carter last minute wherever we decided to dump him.

"The noise?" Paul said. "We're the only ones here."

"Just being careful," I said. "You ready to get in some

exercise?"

Paul complimented my cleanup job with enthusiasm given that I was never a neat freak. My apartment down the street had dishes piled up past the rim of the sink and laundry stacked to the ceiling in my bedroom. However, when others' comfort, or in this case, freedom, were concerned, I could be a true perfectionist.

We were both pathetically out of shape but somehow managed to get Carter down the fire escape and into the trunk of the Alero. I'd sold my Volvo for heroin money. That car had a huge trunk and would've been perfect for this endeavor. But I had put regret out of my mind as I'd cleaned out the Alero and parked it in the alley. The rug and the body barely fit and we had to tie the lid of the trunk shut with a bungee chord.

I suppose when you're disposing of a junkie's body at two a.m. on a Friday night, you can't be too picky.

4

—

AFTER DRIVING AIMLESSLY downtown for about twenty minutes, up and down Broadway then south toward the river until we hit Market Street, Paul finally suggested the all but abandoned Portland docks as an ideal place for, "Carterall disposal" as my comrade in arms adroitly stated. We'd long ago combined the name "Carter" with the word "Adderall," one of the fiend's favorite forms of speed, and come up with the nickname we found hilarious. Tonight, our inside joke brought only a few short laughs.

Portland is the East Los Angeles of Louisville. Despite all the charitable hearts and noble community organizers the city produces each year, the crime rate of the riverside neighborhood continues to skyrocket. Gang initiations multiply. Drive-bys continue to kill innocents, especially children in most cases, for some inexplicable reason.

The sagging shotgun shacks and the pastel colored murals that coated every red brick flood wall seemed to serve as an ad hock Greek chorus as we moved west down Portland Avenue toward the docks.

"What if we're not alone?" Paul asked from the passenger side.

"Then we drive around a little longer." I turned the CD player up to drown out any further Q&A. Steve Earle sang on about weed, whites, and wine. My kind of song.

When we reached 28th St., I steered the Alero left at a darkened body shop named Bud's. Broken-down F-150s and Plymouths with shiny rims sat in the lot waiting for attendance. We drove slowly, passing gutted barred-up liquor stores, a wig shop now out of business, boards nailed over empty window sills, numbers spray painted to note foreclosure.

"So it's come to this." Paul scanned the landscape. A few black kids clocked on the corner in front of a whitewash Cathedral, slinging whatever form of dope was popular on this block.

"Don't make eye contact," I warned Paul.

We arrived at the grassy lot buttressed by park benches that faced the river flowing effortlessly south toward Paducah where it emptied into the Mississippi. "People in Louisville used to be able to get on flatboats and sail straight on to New Orleans." I smiled sadly watching the river flow as I continued my history lesson and Paul at least pretended to listen, humoring his emotionally stunted best friend, knowing I had trouble processing the heavier things in life like death and love. "Those damned flatboats didn't even have power and the city, the state, men of good fortune still found a way to provide an affordable means of inventive river travel that took next to no time at all. Now a guy with a Master's degree can't even afford a date." I took another moment to gaze at the gusted clouds rolling slowly above Portland's smoldering smokestacks farther down the Ohio.

A dead body lay in my trunk and I hadn't even killed the engine or considered the specifics of how we would get Carter in the river. Instead, I stood in front of my car, like a perfect dolt, philosophizing, feeling sorry for myself, my culture, and people like Paul, plagued with the curse of the thinking man. Freedom was our drug, and every day we either lost or forfeited a little more.

"Jon?" Paul had one foot out the door. "This is not the time."

"I'm driving my one shot at owning my own business into the ground and now I'm probably going to go to prison for the rest of my life."

"We are going to drop this little prick in the Ohio and never speak of this again. Grow a pair and get out of the damned car. No one's going to prison. Especially not over Carterall."

I'd been smart enough to stop on Market Street when I spotted two cinder blocks in the front yard of a condemned row house. Paul, an obsessive compulsive stickler for adherence to schedules and plans, had protested against the unannounced setback in travel arrangements. But as we carried the carpet, taped shut, down the narrow, northernmost boardwalk dozens of yards from the shore, he remembered the weights and warmed up to my earlier decision. As if he'd just realized why I'd brought them, his eyes bulged as he spoke. "If we tie those blocks to the carpet and..."

"I know," I said, wheezing as I laid my end of the body bag at the tip of the pier. "Now you're starting to see the big picture."

Paul smiled as he dropped Carter's head to the hardwood, the skull snapping against the boards with a skin crawling crack. "We tie 'em to the rug..."

"...Then we push the rug downriver, let it get further toward the middle of the Ohio before it starts to sink." I wiped the sweat from my brow. I'd grown painfully sober. "It's perfect."

While Paul guarded the body, I walked back to the Alero and retrieved the two cinder blocks, along with the chains I'd found in the same yard. Paul tied one weight to each end of the carpet before we sailed Carter into the softly rushing Ohio, watching the speed fiend sink about five yards down river. We smiled at one another and began walking back toward the car.

5

FOR SOME STRANGE reason, the night after my first murder, I had absolutely no desire to drink or ingest narcotics. While my mind was made up to get clean and make a new stake at things, I could not ignore reality: my body would soon grow deathly ill from withdrawal and concessions would need to be made considering I had responsibilities, a business to run, and weirdoes like Paul who depended on me to give their lives meaning.

There were two choices, cold turkey or tapering, and cold turkey wasn't any kind of choice at all. I didn't want to drive the Alero so soon after the untimely demise of the promising and chipper Carterall. Paul tried to convince me to drive myself to the ghetto to do my dirty work, but I assured him that, in matters of murder, body disposal, and the aftermath, I was convinced the devil lay in the details.

"The Alero is hidden from plain site, Paul," I rubbed at my puffy eyelids while explaining the obvious. "I found a spot that I can only describe as miraculous east of Cherokee on Highland. Like six or seven branches from these massive Magnolia's hang down and completely shield the car from view."

"Why so worried about the car?" The panic I'd worked half an hour the night before to dispel returned to Paul's voice, his baritone cracking with the last word he spoke.

"I'm not particularly worried about the car, Paul." The last thing I wanted was to spend half an hour of my early withdrawal hours convincing Paul that the SS were not coming for us. "I'm just taking extra precautions. To be honest, it's more for your benefit than mine. I know how you'd worry if any T's weren't crossed or I's dotted."

There was a moment of pondering silence, Paul thanking me for my attention to detail, for saving him from even more ulcers and acid indigestion. "Okay. Where do we have to go?"

The trip downtown didn't take long. Paul drove me to the parking lot of the Economy Inn on Main Street where I left him in his Pontiac to idle for a few moments while I traipsed up the stucco steps to room 313 where I bought exactly three orange, octagonal Suboxone pills. By the time we arrived back at the store, the "stop signs" as subs had been nicknamed because of their shape, had dissolved completely under my tongue, the quickest way to force the suckers to hit your system and cease all symptoms and side effects of detox. I breathed easier now that the drug had begun to do its job, but the horrible taste almost made me retch.

"Why do you keep making that ridiculous face?" Paul asked as I winced a twentieth time. Paul pulled into my neighbor's parking place at the bookstore. I scanned the windows of the Grand Victorian to mentally denounce any sign of the two next door yuppies, both law students in their early twenties who drove matching Lexus's. They'd been gone the night before, or at least their sports cars had been missing, but I could get paranoid myself sometimes, and I feared one of them might have been lurking in the shadows somewhere, walking the annoying Chihuahua that never ceased it's howling, watching me and Paul carry Carter's corpse down the fire escape to load it into my trunk.

"I hope I still have some Diet Coke inside." I swallowed a few times hoping the saliva, or just the mere distraction of oral movement, might cause the taste to subside, even momentarily. "Those subs are hell on that palate."

"Well, you're going to have to deal with that on your own." Paul tapped nervously at the dashboard. It had just occurred to me that he hadn't taken the car out of gear or killed the engine. He wasn't coming in. Despite my lack of nausea and uncontrollable bowel movements, a dreary afternoon and evening alone still lay ahead. It was Monday, the only day of the week the bookstore closed.

"What's so important that you can't come in for a beverage?" Just because I'd sworn off alcohol didn't mean my friends had to turn into teetotalers. I had plenty of booze inside and, currently, no one to drink it.

"I got Adam in the morning." Paul was currently unemployed, save the marginal work he did at the bookstore for which I could barely pay enough to justify him even driving over. Adam, his fourteen-year-old son, helped at the store when we needed someone in better shape than me or Paul.

"Well, if it's about Adam..." I said and opened the passenger door just as an LMPD police unit pulled into the space next to Paul's rusted Pontiac. The lights on top shone for just a moment and a single blare of the siren sounded before a massive man with a beer gut the size of East Kentucky exited the driver's side. He was somewhere in his late thirties, early forties, with a thousand-yard stare and a shaved head, a cadence in his posture that told me he'd served in the military, probably killed dozens of innocent children in Iraq only to return to a less than fulfilling law enforcement position in a Midwestern ghetto where he couldn't kill people a tenth as often as overseas.

But what was his reason for bothering us? We'd been parked a good five minutes and hadn't violated any laws of which I knew. When he passed through the Pontiac's headlights on his way to Paul's window, the cop stopped a moment and glared at us through the windshield.

"Dear God." I closed my eyes and tried not to lose bowel control at the sight of the cop's name tag, which read "J. Parrant."

Parrant was Carter's last name.

"What?" Paul's knuckles turned white as he dug his fingertips deep into the steering wheel. "What'd we do?"

I asked Paul if he'd seen the golden nameplate. He hadn't, but before I could alert him to the harsh truth regarding the big cop's namesake, a tapping resounded through the car. Outside Paul's window stood the bearish policeman shining his mag light, illuminating our sallow features, the trash on the passenger floorboards, mostly empty cans of Diet Coca-Cola, Paul's most cherished vice.

Paul rolled the window down and killed the engine.

"You two mind stepping out of the vehicle?" Officer Parrant gazed menacingly at us for a beat before I asked what this was all about. "I mean, we're parked," Paul added.

"I understand that, sir." The cop backed away from the car a few paces and holstered his flashlight. As he did, he took the liberty of opening Paul's door and grinning demurely. "I strongly suggest the three of us take this conversation into the bookstore where we can talk privately."

"About what?" I leaned over Paul's lap and looked the pig in the eye, instantly regretting my decision to do so.

"We can do this the easy way," he said. Then he squatted, getting down on our seated level to stare back at me. "Or we can do this the hard way. The easy way is much... how should I say it... less traumatic than the hard way, boys. Now why don't you do as Mr. Police Officer says, and get the fuck out of the car and into the building so I can enlighten you two a little bit."

6

PAUL AND I were boned.

Officer Jody D. Parrant, who currently sat placidly in one of my armchairs in the reading area of the bookstore, was none other than Carterall's uncle. And, unbeknownst to me or Paul, Carter had told the Officer his intended whereabouts the previous evening.

"And what do you know?" The cop crossed his legs, getting comfortable in my favorite chair, then smiled like a seraph. "The kid never came home that night. His folks are worried sick." The cop removed a small cigar from a tin case in his breast pocket. He didn't ask if I minded if he smoked or not in my building as he lit the cigarillo with my father's golden Zippo he'd seen lying on the coffee table next to him. "Point is," he took a long puff, exuded a thick plume, "I know the kid's a pain in the ass. But he kind of looked up to me." Upon hearing Parrant speak of his nephew in past tense, Paul and I both shared a second's look of stunning defeatism. Then Paul broke the silence with a quickly stifled laugh.

When I looked up, Parrant's smile had only spread wider. He gestured to one of the bar stools to the left of where Paul and I stood, by the window, between the Crime and Western bookcases. "I think you should have a seat."

"I'd prefer to stand." I crossed my arms and leaned

against the post connected to the stairwell.

"You listen to me." Parrant pointed at me with the hand holding the cigarillo. "Carter was supposed to drop a few of those Addies off to his dear old uncle last night. When he didn't show, I cased out your store. I followed you to the river."

So the little rat told his cop uncle about my store, the drugs, everything.

"Are you going to sit now?" Parrant asked.

"In light of this new information," I said, "I definitely don't envision a prolonged visit."

"Seems like it'll either end in arrest or something worse from the way this guy's talking." Paul picked up the Zippo where Parrant had left it and lit a Pall Mall. Then he turned his focus to the pig in our midst. "I just don't understand why the Goon Squad isn't with you? What? Is this like one of those shitty cop movies? You're going to shoot us down like dogs?"

"Listen to me." Parrant bent over and drew a .38 Chief's special from an ankle holster. As he rose he hit Paul in the stomach with the butt of the revolver then trained its barrel on me before I could make a move. Paul crumpled over his lap, cradling his abdomen. He didn't cry out though. The tough old heathen had been through his fair share of mental asylums, county jails, drunk tanks, bar fights, near stabbings, and even dodged a bullet or two since he'd first entered this world on a crisp January morning in Southern Hospital on Dixie Highway.

"You two ever heard of Luther Longmire?" Parrant asked, oscillating the aim on his drop gun between me and Paul.

I nodded "yes." On several occasions I'd gotten tanked at various South End dives and Portland pool halls with the infamous Kentucky gangster. Rumor had it that he'd once bought a police commissioner in the late 1980's who'd gladly taken the fall without naming Luther when IAD started filing charges.

"Me and some of the boys in my precinct are the ones who really run his show. He's just our damn lap dog. We even control his deadliest asset, this one stoop-shouldered, bug-eyed cockroach looking bastard... don't know his real name but everyone calls him Swarthy. Son of a bitch can do more with a buck knife than Legs Diamond could have done with a Thompson submachine gun. So, if for some reason I can't make charges stick or the investigation gets jammed up or takes too long, Luther and Swarthy will be on your ass just to keep me in their good graces."

I'd always considered Luther Longmire a buddy, a drinking buddy mind you, but held a more than negligible level of fondness for the Dixie gangster in my heart. However, I didn't think for a moment he'd chose my side over a dirty cop on the outfit's payroll.

However, I also didn't believe for a moment that this beat cop, or anyone like him, ran Luther's entire outfit.

The cop wanted two thousand a week for his silence, I suppose enough to keep the flagrant disgrace to law and order knee deep in speed, gambling capital, and ethnic underage prostitutes. When he asked if the arrangement was amicable, I simply replied, "Do we have a choice?"

He just laughed.

After he left, Paul watched Parrant's squad car speed west on Highland Avenue, waited for the unit to clear the stop light then turned to me from the office window and declared, "Canada's nice this time of year, I hear."

"Spring's nice everywhere, right?" I eyed the rows of bottles on the wet bar and fought the urge to self-medicate. "I mean everywhere in the western hemisphere."

"It's not nice in places where dirty cops with drop guns want you to turn to nefarious means to supply them with two large a week. Fuck."

"Stop with all that," I said.

"We're through." Paul once again began his pacing, this time along the rows of book display windows and the Crime and Western shelves. "I'll have to abscond with Adam to Canada or resign myself to never seeing my boy again."

"Jesus." I wearily placed a hand over my eyes as to save myself witness to this dramatic charade fit for an Oscar clip.

"All because of that limp-backed pussy Adderall freak you insisted we make a few bucks off every month."

"So this is all my fault?" I blocked his path, forcing him to halt.

"Who else could possibly be to blame?" Paul took a step back, as if so angry with me that proximity constituted the likelihood of violence.

"You were talking about wanting to murder Carter before he even walked through the door. I just happened to accidentally act out your dark desires."

"Here it comes. Justification. Rationalization. They're just like masturbation. We're the only ones that get fucked."

"Let me finish, goddamnit." I closed the space between us, my face centimeters from his. "You've known me a long time. You've known all along what I am and the shitty way I've lived my life. Yet—and I'm grateful, don't get we wrong—you've remained my best friend. When that little bastard came at me last night, you didn't hesitate to knock the hell out of him. And when I accidentally did what I did, you only hesitated momentarily to help me clean up the mess. Well, now we got a brand new mess on our hands."

"You're damn right. A worse one."

"And laying blame ain't gonna help anyone. We're in this together whether you like it or not, and despite where you may believe the fault lies, Parrant is not going to let you slip through the cracks and lay all the alleged debt on me."

"You have a plan?"

"Oh yeah."

"Does it involve a felony?"

"At least four that I can think of off hand."

7

UNLIKE PAUL'S CANADA, one place no one with the correct number of X and Y chromosomes would ever consider nice any time of the year was Cincinnati, Ohio, our destination the day following the blackmail news. Paul hadn't spoken to me since we'd passed the Louisville Metro city limits. The drive from the bluegrass to the Queen City could quite possibly be the most sterile in America; farm houses, barren fields, and Outlet Malls the sum total of the scenery. The two hours it took, driving the speed limit, seemed longer than a cross country trek on a Greyhound. The silence didn't help either.

As my hand moved toward the knob of the radio, Paul curtly ordered me to watch the road. We were driving my Alero as Paul had allowed his ex-wife, who still ran his life, the use of his Pontiac since the Land Rover her new surgeon husband had bought her was in the shop. Normally, I'd give him a mile's length of shit for this, but considering how angry he'd grown with me over the last week, I gave the guy a break.

"I can't keep driving in silence just because you feel put out that we have to take a little road trip today, a road trip that, I might add, will within a week lead to a very large payday."

"A road trip." Paul lit a cigarette, dramatically pausing before exhaling the first halo of smoke, "at the end of which, you will officially be a drug dealer. And all that money in our hands we'll have to turn right over to that douche nozzle beat cop."

Now, I suppose, would be the prudent time to share the plan I'd concocted which, unbeknownst to me at the plan's Genesis, actually served two purposes: importing heroin from Cincinnati, where the drug went for a hundred and fifteen dollars a gram at most, to Louisville, where tar or China White could easily be unloaded for triple that price. My plan, I told myself, might just save the bookstore, which had been in arrears since the day I opened the place. It'd also keep Parrant paid until I figured out a more sadistic and satisfactory way to deal with dirty pig. And if we were to cut it—which considering the purity of Roach's product, selling his dope untouched to Louisville's comparatively virginal bloodstream would make me and Paul murderers—we could easily make a profit and pay Parrant.

"Great example I'm setting for Adam." He lit his twelfth cigarette of the ride. Speaking of his son, I suppose, he skyrocketed into an especially maudlin mood.

"What?" I took one of his cigarettes from the pack on the console behind the gear shift, waited for him to set the lighter down, and lit my own. "You'd rather him take money from that Swahili fuck your wife married?"

"He's Bosnian."

I rolled down the window to let the cool spring morning air drift in and perhaps ice down our tempers. I still couldn't keep from prodding Paul about his ex's new hubby, revenge for the silent treatment he'd given me the entire way up. "So he isn't Swahili. That means he's kind of white for which you can thank your lucky stars. If she was getting the stiff one eye from some black chappy, your imagination would run wild in regards to size and girth and comparing yourself to the big bastard. You'd probably be dead right now from stress and worry. Your kid would be far more multicultural, probably less respectful of your bland Caucasian ways."

"Shut up," he yelled, punching the glove compartment several times until the latch broke. "Shut the hell up. Isn't it enough you've turned me into a murderer and a felon. You have to insult my first born?"

"First born?" I laughed. "What are you, Tony Soprano?"

"I'm about to be." He glanced over, a sardonic smile replacing the grimace he'd been wearing the entire trip. We enjoyed our morning's first echoes of laughter as the Cincinnati skyline appeared, graced with far greater resplendence and grandeur than that of our hometown. Although it was morning, you could still see the afterglow of the blue neon lights that shone so bright upon the city's night children the evening prior. I'd spent many a lost weekend in Cincinnati.

On one of these dope-laden, booze heavy jaunts, as I often engaged in when visiting a city like Cinci known for great heroin, I abandoned a perfectly nice girl at a bar to scour the ghetto for a half-gram. This was the night I met Roach, the most successful peddler and procurer of dope ever encountered in my drug-induced misadventures. The first time I saw him, he was bitch slapping one of his corner boys, a corn-rowed teenager, in front of a chicken joint across from the infamous Bogarts where I'd seen Joe Strummer play four years back. Short Vine Street, the home of Bogarts and the city's best dope, is located in the northernmost enclave of Cinci's worst neighborhood, Over-the-Rhine, the mean streets of which had perhaps been solely responsible for the town's nickname, Nasty Natti. I pulled over and waited for the man who would later introduce himself as Roach to finish his business with the teenager. Violence brings out the worst in most people. Not so with the noble Roach who, when I humbly approached and asked if he was good—drug speak for "Do you have any heroin on you?"—he calmly and quietly appraised me, quickly deciding that I was not a cop or a C.I. The violence he'd perpetuated had put him in a more than amicable mood; he gave me a half gram for sixty dollars, the deal of a Cincinnati lifetime.

Needless to say, Roach and I stayed in touch.

I almost immediately regretted regaling Paul with the story of my introduction to Roach.

"Great." Paul had taken over driving once we crossed the bridge and entered the city proper. "Not only have I allowed you to talk me into dealing drugs, but now I find out the supplier we're trying to court is a blood-lusting psychopath."

I only had a third of the Suboxone left and had promised myself to hold out until I really needed it. I'd brought a change of clothes as to not arrive at our meeting with my shirt pasted to my chest. They say the third day of withdrawal is the worst, but for me, it's always the second.

"You look like shit." Paul sighed. "I can't believe, if

this guy's the kingpin mastermind you describe, that he'd do business with a trembling wreck going through detox right before his very eyes."

Vine Street dipped as we left the best of the Cincinnati skyline behind us and entered Over-the-Rhine. Thanks to the precious, socially conscious children of the baby boomer generation, my old stomping grounds had begun to suffer greatly at the hands of gentrification. My favorite fish joint had been replaced by an art gallery which displayed a nauseatingly pedestrian abstract sculpture of random shapes made of wood and steel glued together and draped with toilet paper.

"I remember when this was a nice place to come." I broke the Suboxone in half, let the half-pill dissolve under my tongue. I felt a little more comfortable in my own skin.

"What are you talking about?" Paul shifted gears as we ascended another incline, leaving behind the rows of tenements and Italianate walk-ups, many left still gutted from the previous decade's race riots. "This place is a shithole."

"I always loved it," I told him. "It looks exactly like I feel."

8

ROACH HELD COURT inside the same chicken joint across from Bogart's where, out front, I'd seen him beat down his teenage employee who I later found out had accepted fake bills for a half-gram and hadn't even noticed until the boss took his cut at the end of the night. King's Chicken had been a chain for years in Cinci until the late nineties when ownership changed and the new cokehead proprietor ran most of the business into the ground. Roach, in his infinite benevolence, bought the place, saving the last location on Short Vine. One time, the new kingpin of King's Chicken told me he'd only paid five grand for the place. It turned out, the owner owed Roach big on coke and oxies and with the debt taken into account, only around ten grand remained payable for the business. "Why'd you only give him five then?" I'd asked Roach. "Because I gave him a discount for the next few months on his dope," Roach had laughed, "but cut the shit out of every bag I gave him so I'd still come out ahead."

The number one rule in hustling, Roach had informed me, was to always come out ahead. Give nothing away. And make sure you're never the one getting screwed, because in the game, someone always winds up with the short straw.

The inside of King's hadn't changed over the last

decade. Bright orange blinded the customer, from the Formica counter and booths, to the wall paint and cracked tiles. Roach sat on his throne at the counter at the opposite end of the register, puffing on a Newport in blatant disregard of the smoking ban and texting someone on his cell. When the bell rang as Paul and I entered, he finished his phone business in a matter of seconds and removed his Reds cap as he rose, rubbing at his shiny bald crown. He stood six foot two and carried his two hundred plus pounds well, most of it muscle with the recent addition of a small gut thanks to Budweiser and middle age. For a dope dealer, Roach was ancient at thirty-five years old. The majority didn't live to see twenty-seven, but again, he was smarter than most. He drove a minivan and avoided dressing in anything that resembled generic Ghetto gangster regalia. He wore brand new dark blue jeans, a dress shirt, and a houndstooth coat: a respectable looking black businessman to anyone who didn't know him. He avoided petty posturing and turf disputes, the bread and butter of most aspiring thugs, but punished disloyalty and negligence as severely as Scarface.

"You look like shit." Roach, never one to mince words, placed an arm around my shoulder and twirled me into a bear hug, lifting me off the ground and whispering, "But then again, I figured you'd be dead by now, so I guess looking shitty is a pleasant surprise in some ways."

Paul shifted his weight from one foot to the other in quick rhythm and scratched at his chin, breathing loud, reminding me to hurry up and make the introductions. I stood aside and ushered Paul in my place for he and

Roach to grow acquainted. Roach offered his fist. Paul stared quizzically at the clenched hand a few seconds before making his own fist and bumping Roach's, Paul's hand missing the entire massive square of flesh save a few knuckles. Roach chortled and placed his palm over his mouth and goatee to spare us and any passers-by from stray spittle. "You all too much. I guess the world best get ready for the Revenge of the Nerds." Then he lowered his voice and said to both of us, "Looks like the chess team be taking over the dope game in Louisville."

"What I don't understand," Roach broke his speech to wash down the bite of short ribs he'd just eaten with a swig from his plastic to-go cup of Sprite, "is why now?"

"What do you mean why now?" It was the second time Paul had spoken, the other when he gave his name. Roach just looked at him as if my friend had talked out of turn, hadn't waited for the conch shell to pass his way.

"Now's as good a time to make money as any." I broke the staring contest between my best friend and my favorite heroin dealer.

"True." Roach nodded piously to the almighty dollar. "Now before we continue on to numbers and weight, we going to step over to the Blockbuster parking lot on the corner and I'm gonna take some security measures."

Paul's brow furrowed and the first of many sweat beads began raining from his pores I could see the wheels turning in his mathematical mind. The guy's gonna kill us.

To great hilarity, Roach also noticed the fever on the newbie white man, crowing and slapping his knee.

"Calm down, Charles Grodin." Roach liked calling white men Charles Grodin, as if he served as the epitome of everything generically Caucasian.

"Relax." I told Paul. "If he was going to kill us we wouldn't have gotten past downtown."

We were patted down in the Blockbuster parking lot, between a brand new Cadillac SUV and the guard rail. The dirty job was done by one of Roach's underlings, a project teen who suffered from an obvious degree of hero worship in regards to his boss. The master of ceremonies then ordered me and Paul to enter the Caddy's back seat. I assured Paul again that we would not be killed.

"Why would he have patted us down?" I whispered to Paul. The logic seemed to afford him some relief.

The teenager drove. Roach road shotgun. Paul and I remained silent in the back seat. The doors stayed locked. We took 71 across the river, back into Kentucky. The kid descended the Covington exit and suddenly the drab highway surroundings gave way to a canopy of Cypress trees on a street lined with Grand Victorians, some of them connected. Paul kept nudging me as if I had answers. All I knew was that Roach didn't want us knowing where he kept his weight for longer than it took to drive to the dope.

I didn't blame him.

The kid steered us past the picturesque residential streets sheltered by the branches of towering oaks that met directly above the avenue's dividing line. The Grand Victorians and perfectly manicured begonias ceased and we entered the slums on Covington's easternmost bend in the river, where the tourists couldn't see, where White Castles and liquor stores dominated the economy. The kid pulled up to a white shotgun shack on a side street, the weeds overgrown, the paint peeling, ancient newspapers stacked on the front porch.

I whistled. "You didn't have to book the Ritz for our little meet and greet, Roach."

"We park on the street and go around back, okay?" Roach looked back at me and Paul, ignoring my sarcasm.

We were dropped off on the corner. Roach ordered the kid to park on the street and wait. He called the teen by the name Ty. I needed to shake the mindset that this was a normal growing boy working for our hopefully soon-to-be supplier. At sixteen, or however far in age he'd somehow managed to reach tiptoeing through the landmine of American ghettos his entire life, Ty likely already "had a few bodies on him," as Roach said of those who'd committed multiple homicides. Ty confirmed my suspicions with the lifeless stare he shot me as I exited the vehicle.

"I don't think that kid likes us very much." Paul attempted small talk with Roach as we ambled up the small incline through the weeds that ran along the side of the house.

"He don't warm up to most people." Roach unlocked the side door of the shotgun shack. Inside, two gutted couches made a V facing a fireplace full of ancient ash and crumpled pages of the *Cincinnati Enquirer*. The only light came from the overcast day outside, from the open doorway and the cracked and broken blinds.

"Funny thing about Ty," Roach said, shutting the door behind us and standing in it's way with his arms crossed, blocking any quick exit Paul and I may have considered. "That boy don't got to be told nothing twice. The other day for example, I got word one of my boys been talking to the police. White boy out of Clifton. Handled all the college business I could stand. I found out the rumor was true. Boy was a motherfucking snitch." Roach stepped a few paces toward the fireplace where Paul and I listened, dangling on every word as if he were our hangman.

"That's not cool." My voice broke as I tried to reassure Roach that these two white boys were, in fact, not snitches. Why is it, innocent or not, you always act guilty when a big scary sociopath is grilling you? There seemed to be no right mode of behavior when accused of betrayal, especially when the man accusing you has no qualms with dispensing human life, and no rules or regulations, like with police, to guide him.

"I'm glad you agree with my stance on snitches." Roach rested his back against the door and grinned. "Because I chose your new friend Ty to deal with him. You see, this snitch was the lowliest of junkies. Whored his own fiancée out so he could stay well. All Ty had to do was call the motherfucker, tell him we had some new shit and needed it tested and when the fiend showed up to this very house," Roach pointed to the floorboards, making it clear the murder had been committed where we now stood, "he handed college boy a 30 gauge syringe filled with a little dope and a shit load of rat poison. Made the little junkie kill his own self." Roach stood

53

and took two paces toward me and Paul, still standing at the fireplace, both of us now breathless. "So you see how I deal with disloyalty." Roach grimaced in Paul's direction then shot me a far more sterile glare. "You still want to do business?"

I'd sold my prize Vincent Black Lightning I'd been restoring for five years to pay for this dope load and Paul had cleared out his sparse savings. This expenditure had left me just enough to shut the landlord up for another week about the late rent I owed. I smiled and shook Roach's hand. "I want to do business with you today. And I hope I'll have many more trips to Cincinnati. This could be the beginning of a beautiful friendship."

"Friends?" Roach chortled. "You got a thing or two to learn about the dope game using words like friends. Friends and money ain't got nothing to do with one another, cuz."

"I hope you're happy." Paul and I sat on my sagging couch, side by side, me measuring quarter-grams of dope on the electronic scale we'd bought at a Bardstown Road head shop on our way home, Paul chain smoking and worrying, his favorite past time. To the right of the dope and scales were two boxes of sandwich bags and a plastic dispenser of coffee mate, what I'd use for cut. If we sold this dope pure on the streets of Louisville, a blossoming heroin mecca, there would be a dozen overdoses our first day in business. Plus, cutting the product exponentially increased profits. With any luck, we could unload the bulk or maybe even all of what we'd bought on my most dependable Louisville dealer, Rig.

"A bloodthirsty lunatic now has our number." Paul stepped into my kitchenette and killed the cherry of his Pall Mall with sink water, tossing the butt atop my overflowing garbage bin. "Does he know all about you, Jon? The bookstore? Your address?"

"Calm down, man." The dope weighed right. I knew it would. Roach might be a lot of things. Roach was a killer, perhaps even a sadist. But I'd never pegged him as a cheat or a liar. He knew the eternal truths of men living a life of crime, one of the most important: to live outside the law you must be honest. "First of all, you could stop your bitching and help me weight these. I mean, you know how goddamn hard it is to kick dope. And here I sit, looking at more heroin than I've ever seen in one place."

"Oh, spare me." Paul sat on the futon across from the couch and placed his face in his hands. When he looked up from his state of repose, his features had softened. He regretted what he'd said, knowing from watching me struggle for years that I was fighting off hell and damnation.

"I'm sorry." Paul stuck his hands in his leather waistcoat and laid down on the futon, staring blankly at the ceiling. "I just can't believe things have gotten this fucked. I'm basically unemployed. My ex-wife is such a back stabbing, insufferable shithead that I have to bite my lip and sit on my hands to avoid ripping her intestines out through her big ass."

"Sheila's ass got big?"

"Big time." Paul laughed for a change. "I guess you haven't seen her in a few years."

"Why would I want to see your bitch ex-wife? I mean it was hard enough putting up with her the last year of your marriage. Do I have to do penance for your poor choices in relationships?"

"Soon enough, none of this will matter. We'll both be in chains at the bottom of the Ohio just like Carter, only further north, closer to Roach's neck of the woods."

"Can't you even attempt to look on the bright side?" I walked across the living room littered with empty bottles and take out containers to steal one of Paul's cigarettes off the glass coffee table, taking a break from the scales and the dope packaging. I'd quit smoking the same year I opened the bookstore, half a decade ago, the same year I'd gotten on junk. For some strange reason, despite the cornucopia of other mind-altering substances I'd been pumping into my body on a daily basis for nearly half a decade, while I still snuck in a rogue cigarette every so often, I'd never returned to my pack-a-day habit. Now seemed like as good a time as any.

I finished weighing the product at the bar then turned to explain to Paul our next move. I prayed he wouldn't have a coronary.

9

IT'S POSSIBLE. IF you come from wealth, to live in
Louisville for a lifetime and never have to see the slums.
My father told me the city, to this day, remained one of
the most blatantly segregated he'd ever seen. Roy Wilkins
Boulevard downtown is the clear line of demarcation
that separates the middle class and wealthy, mostly
white, from the underclass, mostly black. Old Louisville,
the historic neighborhood just to the southeast of Roy
Wilkins, had begun to degenerate over the past decade
with the destruction of the Clarksdale Projects. Still,
the majority of all crime, murders and drug trafficking
especially, occurred in the West End, from Wilkins all
the way to the river. This is why, if you happen to make
the poor life choice of ever trying heroin, and happen
to be white, you will find yourself quickly adapting to
a severe change in scenery, for you will be spending
more than half your waking hours passing pawn shops
and check cashing joints on your way to meet the dope
man in the bathroom of a cash only greasy spoon or the
parking lot of a housing project. I hate to admit it, but
when I was growing up in St. Matthews, a predominantly
white, middle to upper class burg in the far east end,
despite dealing with my demonic drunk of a father on
a daily basis, I'd built no grit to prepare for my fear
of poorer neighborhoods. However, the first time I

was dope sick and my dealer couldn't come my way, I fearlessly ventured to Vermont Avenue, a street lined with cars on cinder blocks and corner boys cat calling at the passing women. Vermont Avenue was considered the worst street in the worst part of the city, located in the River Park neighborhood, ten blocks west of the dividing line.

After that trip, my fear of the ghetto began to depreciate daily.

Unfortunately, Paul had undergone no such experience.

"At least I can act a bit more cultured if we make it back alive," Paul said as I put the Alero in park on the corner of Vermont and Bank in front of a crumbling Victorian home that had likely been owned by prosperous and pasty southern gentlemen fifty years before white flight and busing.

"Who are we meeting again?" Paul pulled out his Pall Malls. I held out my hand to bum one of his smokes. He rolled his eyes and handed one over then lit fire to both.

"We're meeting my main connect in Louisville." I took a long drag as I rolled down both windows in the front seat. "He'll call when he pulls up. This is how it works. Being a junkie or a drug dealer... well, both positions have a lot in common with private detective work. A lot of waiting in parked cars."

"You learn something new every day."

"If you want to jump ship, be my guest. Just don't rat me out when Officer Parrant sends you to LaGrange."

I acted like I'd only entered the dope game out of necessity. Who was I kidding, though? I knew even then that the reason this recent detox had been so manageable was because a new addiction had begun to enter my life, power. I'd tasted a bit of the sweet nectar with my posh, quasi-Parisian Gertrude Stein-esque salon disguised as a used bookstore. While I'd yet to see any return on what Paul had dubbed our "extra-legal" investment, the images of pomp and glory, hundred-year-old wine and orgies danced in my head like the strippers I planned hiring to do nothing more than lounge around my mansion and the swimming pool outside.

Every time I had this fantasy a call from Irina would come in, like clockwork. She seemed to sense from miles away my larcenous heart wandering astray again. When my cell vibrated in the cup holder underneath the car radio, I glanced at the number on the screen, already confident who would be on the other line.

"Shit." I said. "Shit, shit, shit."

"What?" Paul began panicking again. He wouldn't stop shaking his leg which in turn caused the hole car to wobble. Motion sickness had begun to set in but, requesting he cease would be pointless. "Is it him? Is that a text or something saying he thinks we're not legit, that we're cops? Drive off, man."

"Shut up," I snapped. "You act like you've never seen a black person before. Why don't you act as liberal as you vote." The phone rang a third time. "It's Irina. I haven't talked to her since.... you know."

"No. Since what?"

"Since I killed the son of a bitch who was harassing her. And she always knows when something's up with me. Lately, a lot that she doesn't know has been up and I'm not looking forward to getting called out."

Another ring.

"Just don't answer it," Paul said.

"I don't need this shit."

"So send her ass straight to voice mail. I need you focused."

Pretty soon the ringing would stop anyway and she'd likely text me something shitty.

"I'm gonna take this just to cool her off a little," I said.

The call, suffice to say, did not go well.

"Missing?" Irina shrieked into the phone. "I tell you what he did. You go all stone-cold Steve Austin on me and hang up the phone and now there's an article in the Courier about the missing prince of Anchorage."

I almost regurgitated right then and there. Carter was from the nauseatingly wealthy suburb of Anchorage, but no one in town, especially none of the gossiping adulterers at Owl Creek Country Club, would ever consider the little doper a prince.

I heaved a purposeful, dramatic sigh before continuing. Irina seemed to thrive on those, for better or worse. "Carter was... is an utter menace to his friends, family and neighbors, a philistine of biblical proportions whose only cultivated trades seem to be inconveniencing others and bringing grief to people who don't need anymore. The asshole probably just left to find a city with a cheaper drug market."

"What happened, Jon?" she asked.

I pulled the cell away from my ear.

"I know something is up with you. Why can't you talk to me? Are you using again? Starting your mornings with a breakfast of beer and whiskey? You are going to

60

wind up dead or in jail."

"I'm actually sober, believe it or not."

"How about not? How about I just assume you're lying since most of the time you are."

She continued her judgments and chastisement while I held the phone away from my ear so I didn't have to hear her exact words. I looked at Paul and made the yada-yada symbol, clicking the tip of my index finger against my thumb to imitate a mouth opening and closing. Even though there was an inch between the receiver and my ear, I could still make out the basics of her lecture. She felt lied to, left out, and worst of all, worried about me and the possible consequences of whatever I'd perpetrated.

"You mean you're worried about blow back?" I said into the phone.

"Blow what..."

"I meant... you know... stuff coming back to..."

"Blowjobs? You're talking blowjobs at a time like this?"

"That's not what I meant. Blow back doesn't..."

"Oh, you sick bastard. At a time like this your actually trying to talk dirty, solicit fellatio during..."

"Question," I turned to Paul. "Doesn't soliciting involve money being exchanged?"

"You pay for it one way or another, brother." Paul flicked a cigarette out the window. "I mean, look at the shit she's making you eat simply for trying to do the right thing and keep her from bother during her precious study time."

"I can hear you two." Irina gave me one of her best Bette Davis standoff sighs. "I can hear everything you

61

two are saying."

There was a tap on the passenger window.

Three very angry looking black youths dressed in identical black jeans, T-shirts and low slung toboggans stood on the sidewalk staring at us with the fury of a thousand cuckolded husbands. The oldest stood closest to the window, fists clenched.

"I'm going to have to call you back." I hung up on Irina, fairly certain it was the last time I would talk to her. Or to anyone else in this world.

10

I DIDN'T RECOGNIZE the three rough looking urban youths that stood waiting on the curb outside the passenger door, obviously waiting for us to explain why we'd entered their territory unannounced. Apparently from the hateful appraisal each of them seemed to give Paul's Pontiac, we'd added insult to injury, actually parking our car and spending more than a matter of seconds on their turf.

"This sucks." I sighed and closed my eyes. For some reason, a brief revery of better times graced me, a fragile calm already fading before an inevitable storm.

On weekends, Paul played at a roadhouse on the edge of town called The Air Devil's Inn. Any night after ten the crowd resembled the front row of a Willie Nelson show. The patrons consisted of hippies, bikers, off-duty cops dressed in faded denim and leather, tired of living vicariously through their charges. I'd witness Paul crow a high-lonesome rendition of "I Can't Help It (If I'm Still in Love with You)" that brought tears to the eyes of Luther Longmire, the dive's owner owner and the biggest marijuana distributor in Kentucky. He also dabbled in cocaine and methamphetamine and allegedly sponsored dirty cop's like Carterall's uncle.

Air Devil's is where I met Luther. But we'd never discussed anything but bourbon and hardcore country music, arguing which albums to take on a desert island if we were only allowed five. We differed on one artist, Loretta Lynn. He insisted that, Loretta, talented though she was, automatically disqualified herself by making the grave error of having a vagina. "Women don't make my list unless it's a list that includes penetration and fellatio." While Luther was a blowhard and kind of a jerk-off, I enjoyed talking to him. He put on no airs and treated his friends like royalty, even if he was a sadistic, sexist, racist drug dealer.

I'd never thought to approach Longmire with the dope because, at that time, I thought he was just a legitimate business owner who liked to get his friends high. If I'd gone to him first, a lot of people might still be alive. Of course, others died because of him. At the end of the day, splitting hairs over the wake of dead gets complicated and exhausting. If I'd done A so and so would still be alive, but Frick and Frack would've had to die.

The man I chose to help us disperse our new product went by the street name Rig. He'd always done right by me, even fronted me up to a hundred dollars in heroin when I was sick and broke, letting me pay it off a bit at a time. He'd wanted me to work for him for years. Rig had no connections in Cinci and often encouraged me to make a run up north and bring him back some of that "good nasty 'Natti Ron," as he put it. "Ron" was another street name for heroin. He had no rap sheet, had never gone to the penitentiary or even been jailed. He was, without a doubt, the most careful and successful dealer in town, Louisville's answer to Roach.

My memories of laughing times with Luther Longmire

at the Devil's Inn and of Rig's charity were quickly interrupted by the hateful young men outside.

The tallest, stoutest of the three corner boys, was tapping on Paul's window with a fist the size of a sledgehammer head. I'd hate to be on the receiving end of a blow delivered with that hand. It looked like things were headed in that very direction though.

"What seems to be the problem, sir?" Paul's voice cracked, speaking to the street kid the exact same way any white man would address a cop during a traffic stop. I couldn't help but laugh.

"What seems to be the problem?" the leader of the group mimicked Paul, emphasizing the nasally tone with the same flawless diction that Richard Pryor used in his stand-up to impersonate lame Caucasians. Then he switched back to his street talk. "First off, your boy over there," the shaved headed master of ceremonies nodded in my direction, "seems to think this shit funny."

"I think he was laughing at me," Paul clarified.

"Whatever the fuck he laughing at he need to shut his cocksucker when I'm talking. You see, this here is my corner. And you been loitering. What? You think that just because this is the ghetto you can sit here all you want." He stepped closer to the passenger door, his feet now on the pavement. "Wrong, motherfucker." Then, in one fluid motion, he reached through the window sill and opened the car door from inside. The leader grabbed Paul by his coat lapel, braced him against the car and began choking him out.

"Wait." I exited the driver's side and spoke over the car top. "Let's just cool down one second."

"One more step, Bruce Springsteen." The shorter thug to the leader's left had already trained a hand cannon on me. But despite gunpoint, I couldn't help but ask, "Bruce Springsteen? Do you call all white people Bruce Springsteen?"

"You white." The leader's armed lieutenant thumbed down the hammer of the nickel-plated .45 pointed right at my solar-plexus. "You wearing denim. Close enough to Bruce Springsteen to me."

Paul giggled nervously, the kind of laugh one let's escape when assuming others were about to join in the mirth. "I don't even like Bruce Springsteen, fellas."

The leader chortled and his minions followed suit. "White man don't like Bruce Springsteen? That's like a nigga saying he don't like Indie's." Indies was an all night chicken joint on Eleventh and Broadway. The owners, a Korean couple, only dealt in cash and had made a chain that reached all the way to Bowling Green. It served the best fried food I'd ever tasted.

"Guys, guys, guys." I held my hands in surrender as I approached the curb and stood next to Paul. "Let's not stereotype here. That's not going to help anything or anybody. But I like Indie's too. You see, we're not that different. Maybe we can help each other." I was ready to hand over these guys the dope just to get them to let us drive out of there alive.

"Russell." The one with the gun addressed the leader. "These boys look like they need some help. Let's give 'em some help."

"Help 'em realize we sling the dope in this hood." You east end bitches don't be coming onto our streets taking money out of our pockets, food out our mouths."

How the hell did they know we were bringing heroin in? I had yet to even make my offer, our lives in exchange for several marginally cut grams of china white straight out of Cinci.

We'd been ratted out. It couldn't have been Rig. He was the one who told me if I was ever looking to make a move, come to him first. Why would he encourage me to do business, then have me executed?

As Rig's Black Escalade with the tinted windows, pulled in front of the First Immanuel Church a few yards away from where Paul and I stood at gunpoint, I figured all would be revealed soon enough. Thug Number Two lowered his hand cannon after an authoritative glance from Russell who, just to let Rig know the nature of the situation, tucked his shirt tail behind the butt of a 9mm Browning stuffed in his waistband.

Two black men, somewhere in their late twenties or early thirties, both heads shaved, stepped down from the driver's side of the SUV. One drew a bright silver Beretta but kept it dangling loosely at his side as he joined his slightly younger compatriot who had just opened the front passenger door. Rig exited the back seat slowly, one foot several seconds ahead of the other, like a king stepping down from his chariot.

Rig, like Roach, didn't dress in the modern giveaway garb that might as well have DRUG DEAL stenciled all over the denim and leather. He kept his natty hair short, almost as close cropped as a crew cut, wore black dress pants, a white Gucci suit shirt, leather duster, and spit-shined Italian loafers.

"Russell, why you gotta be stepping out of your area of expertise?" Rig crossed his arms, scratched his beard then glanced back at the younger bangers who'd just been holding me and Paul hostage. "Why you gotta pull car jacks—on East End white boys to boot—when I am more than generous with the streets and corners I let you clock on?"

"This ain't no car jack." The one who'd been leveling the piece on us informed Rig.

"Anybody talking to you?" Russell snapped at his lieutenant then shifted his gaze back to Rig. "Sorry bout that. Young bloods, you know how they be. Young, dumb, and full of cum."

"If this ain't no car jack, what it is it Russell?"

"I got word these two bringing Ron onto my streets like they own the fuckin' place."

"Your streets?" Rig laughed.

"Give me a goddamn break. I know who I kick up to. But they're my streets to supervise."

"Just watch your wording on things. As it so I happens, I know these two, so they aight. Unless you hear otherwise, they can pass from now on."

"No worries."

"How'd you know we had dope?" I asked Russell, an almost immediately regrettable decision.

Russell and Rig spoke in unison: "What?"

I turned to Rig and said lowly, "Man, they didn't just know we were dealing in the abstract. They know we're holding right now. And they were gonna take us. How'd they know? And why weren't you consulted first? If they knew we were holding, how did they NOT know who we were bringing it to? And if they knew that, why'd they stop us? Think about it."

Rig's eye's got as big as poker chips. He stared down Russell for a moment that seemed an hour before Russell finally said, "Man, this just bidness. We heard some shit. We didn't know they was bringing you nothing."

Then they shared an almost psychic exchange, a transpiration neither Paul nor I could understand at the moment. Rig tried to shrug it off, his features softening as he stretched the muscles in his neck. "Get in the car," he said to his two men, then to us, "You two follow."

As soon as Rig began to turn, Russell drew the Browning and shot him in the throat. As if expecting some flagrant act of betrayal from a man of Russell's nature, Rig had already pulled his Glock. Rig stumbled for cover behind the Escalade. He let off three shots before he found safe haven. One of the hollow points found purchase in Russell's gut. The Judas grabbed his stomach and headed down the block, leaving his lieutenants to their own fates. Both of Rig's men had begun firing back at Russell's boys. Paul and I stood frozen as shots sparked off his car top and the cement at our feet. Unarmed and lost in the middle of gang warfare, our muscles had been made impotent by the slaughter before us.

By the time the smoke had cleared, both of Russell's men looked like hamburger helper and only one of Rig's boys remained standing, the older one. I remembered his street name, D, from my many years of dealings with Rig's crew. D blew the smoke from the barrel of his .38 then he, Paul, and I approached the wounded leader. Rig tried in vein to stop the arterial spray the flowed from his neck, using both hands to slow the copious blood pour.

"Where Russell?" Rig somehow spoke a throaty gargle.

"Where Russell?" D repeated. "Man, he run down the fuckin' street. I'm more concerned with your shot up ass."

"D," Rig choked, "you dumb piece of shit. Cain't you see I obviously ain't gonna make it. I just wanna make sure Russell don't neither."

"He raises a very decent point," Paul said. As a reward for his insight, Rig tucked his bloody Glock in Paul's palm then spoke his last words to D. "Chase that motherfucker down to make sure he gets got." Not exactly the most elegiac verse to ever grace my ears, but then again, Rig was never a man who worried himself with flowery prose.

Rig's lights had gone out. A single tear descended from D's right eye. He told us, "You heard the man. We can't ignore ol' Rig's last wishes."

"How far you think he's gotten?" I asked D.

"I know he getting' farther us standing around talking about him."

We stared down the street at the blood trail Russell had left. It forked right, across the road, toward a parking lot behind a flower shop that had long ago gone out of business. Wrong neighborhood for romance, I suppose. Although from the way the day had turned, funerals seemed to be a growth industry. Perhaps the shop owners hadn't marketed to the correct demographic.

"If we drive we'll make it to that parking lot quicker." D slid across the hood of Rig's Escalade and entered the driver's side.

"Well," I said to Paul, who just stood there in front of the Baptist Church staring at dead men on the sidewalk, "get in the goddamned car."

I took the passenger seat. Paul sat in the back, in the middle. D sped down Vermont and peeled into the parking lot of the now defunct Dougie's Flowers. Like crimson bread crumbs, Russell had left a trail all the way to a parked cherry apple red Ford Avenger. When the car screeched to a halt, I only got half a glance at Russell, his driver's door open. He'd almost made it.

Then the window had suddenly rolled down and D started shooting. Russell's rib cage opened and he slumped down the leather of the car door's interior, one hand clinging to the steering wheel as if it were life support.

We all exited the Escalade, to stand over the dying Russell, his Browning too many feet away from his near breathless body to do him any good. D pointed with his gun at Russell's face and said to me and Paul, "Your turn, playas." His gold grill shone in the morning sun as he grinned cheek to cheek.

"Is that really necessary?" Paul smiled back.

D hung his head, the fat of his coal black skin touching the upper rim of his wife beater. He chortled. Then, quicker than he'd let his head go low, looked up and drew down on Paul, telling my friend and I, "Y'all witness me and mine get some blood on our hands here today. Now Rig liked you. But I don't know you. I need insurance."

My eyes oscillated back and forth between the dying

71

King of Vermont Avenue and the newly crowned Regent of the West End. We had no choice. To survive this, Paul and I both had to put a bullet in Russell. I was trying to roll with the punches. But turns of fate such as this made me wonder if they'd ever stop.

"Okay." D rolled his eyes. "Let me make it real simple for y'all. You each put one in diabolical mastermind here, or I kill all three of you and let the cops figure out what happened."

Without another thought, looking away from the dying man below, I picked up Russell's Browning and, aiming vaguely for the dying dealer's face, pulled the trigger. I turned away from whatever damage the hollow point had done.

Paul aimed the bloody Glock Rig had handed him and glanced at D for approval. The gangster nodded encouragingly. I pushed Paul back a few feet to save his nice clothes from the arterial spray. Paul pointed the barrel at Russell's face, turned away as I had, then fired.

We handed our murder weapons over to D and hurried away. We managed to avoid facing what we'd left in the parking lot of Dougie's Flowers.

11

D ORDERED ME and Paul to ride with him in Rig's SUV over the Second Street Bridge into Jeffersonville where I would rent us a pay-by-the-week motel room. "Safe place for us to get our stories straight, regroup. Line things out now that the big man's with the bigger man upstairs," D said. Before we left, D and I got in Paul's Pontiac with him and moved it three streets away from the crime scene. Paul used an old sweatshirt to wipe the blood off the hood in case the cops canvassed the area.

As we sped out of the West End in the late Rig's Escalade, sirens from the east grew eardrum-piercingly loud. We'd barely escaped the police's arrival.

When we got to the motel, D stretched out on the bed. Paul and I took the sofa chairs that surrounded the circular table by the window. D stretched another moment then rose to place the case he'd brought in with him on his lap. He thumbed a combination code on his metal attache case until it opened. Mounds of cash, scales, a 9mm Beretta and two huge Ziploc bags of heroin made up the basic contents.

D went on about how it must have been the other lieutenant, Randall, the one who'd died on Vermont Avenue, who, along with Russell and company, turned on Rig and informed of our new business venture. "Motherfucker never seemed right. Shady and shifty. I'm glad the bitch is dead." I bet he was. No one to contest the accusation. I didn't know if D was behind the setup or not, but I did know that he had money, we had dope, and I had bills to pay. No time for sentimentality. This was business.

However, if he was behind the betrayal, how long before he decided Paul and I were liabilities?

"Let me see the shit." D said.

I reached inside my denim jacket and brought out the two neatly folded manilla envelopes tossing them next to the case. I looked back at Paul who sat with his hand clasped as if in a prayer on the circular table.

"Hey," I said to Paul.

He just stared, comatose, at the green floral design of the floor.

I snapped my fingers before his face. "Hey," I said louder.

Paul looked up, the color long gone from his face. He no doubt still saw Russell dying before us in the flower shop parking lot.

"You got a little something..." I pointed to my own hand, indicating the dried blood spatter on Paul's wrist and fingers.

Paul examined his hands as a woman would applying fingernail polish. "Jesus Christ."

He made a b-line for the bathroom.

"How come you already bag these up?" D pointed to the two dozen or so baggies of heroin.

"Just trying to make your job easier I suppose." I tipped my toboggan toward him, dignified-like.

"Thanks?" He looked at me as if I were a perfect

buffoon. "I guess."

While Paul dry heaved in the bathroom, D scooped as many baggies as he could onto the small electronic scales. I twiddled with my thumbs and paced the room, then thought of a factor no one had brought up as we'd all been distracted by the overall carnage we'd left behind in Louisville.

"Who is going to test this?" I stopped in my tracks, facing the parking lot and the first drops of rain clinging to the window.

"What?" he asked, mouthing the numbers that appeared on the scales' screens.

"I mean the way this whole process works, if I'm correct, is, besides the whole weighing thing, you guys have to test the dope to see to its purity, correct? I mean Rig used to call me all the time to test his new shit. I was his go-to guy."

"So you test it." D shrugged, still looking at the scales and writing down figures on a yellow note pad.

I shook my head "no." "That's not a good idea, man."

"You a dope fiend, right?" D dropped the last baggie on the pile then stared at me confused.

"I quit," I said with a strange mix of guilt and wounded junkie pride.

"Man." D rose from the bed and rolled his eyes, placing his hands on his hips. "You picked a bitch of a time for that, nigga."

"My bad."

"That's right it's your bad. Now we gotta call someone and get his or her no good ass over here to try this shit. And I gotta rack my brain to think of someone, other than you, who is gonna be honest, and not tell me the shit is just okay so I won't cut it to death."

"Is this how you talk about me when I'm not around?"

For the briefest moment, D appeared ashamed of his lack of character and decorum. "I tell you shit to your face."

I let my cold gaze work on the gangbanger's broken code of honor. "We don't have time to get into all this touchy feely bullshit. Who we going to call to test this dope? You sure you don't want just one more shot before you hang up your spurs?" D shifted his focus to the heroin on the bed.

"I can't." I began searching through my cell phone for an honest junkie. "I have work to do."

12

JIMMY O'HEARN GOT clean and sober for ten years, abstaining from any illicit substances all throughout his twenties. When he hit thirty though, he plummeted from the water wagon so hard everyone who knew him including me started expecting the dreaded phone call informing us that the fall had killed him. I suppose during that decade of sobriety he'd been saving up for the bender that, within ten months after his relapse, landed him in LaGrange doing three years flat for trafficking cocaine, marijuana and heroin.

But Jimmy had never dealt a drug in his life.

He just kept large quantities in his Midland Avenue apartment for parties and personal use. His big mistake had been allowing another junkie, a girl he was sleeping with, and her jealous boyfriend, to see his stash. When the couple got picked up for shoplifting, the boyfriend who'd been pimping out his girl for years, told the cops Jimmy's address in exchange for a walk on the shoplifting charges, knowing the narco squad would find enough weight in the Midland loft to constitute a trafficking charge.

There went Jimmy's job as executive of advertising at one of the biggest PR firms in Louisville, along with his fiancée and the respect of his family and most of his friends. He told me that I was the only person besides his parents who wrote him or visited him during his sentence.

He was the most loyal, honest junkie I'd ever known.

Jimmy had been released a week ago and, from what he'd confessed during our phone conversation, was already back on the needle.

"He was just mad because I never paid for it with his woman."

Jimmy tucked the tips of his long strands of dirty blonde hair behind his ears then mixed the light brown heroin with water in a plastic spoon on the desk by the hotel window. Less than a week out of the joint, and Jimmy looked like a junkie's junky. He wore a dress shirt with the sleeves torn off and jeans stained so heavily, smelling so musky, that they could have stood up on their own and assisted Jimmy with his shot.

"Well, you gave her dope," I pointed out. "You always pay for it one way or another." I winked at Paul, quoting what he'd said in the car before we'd both shot a man's face off. Paul rolled his eyes, finding no amusement in the sick situation we'd willingly entered.

"What?" Jimmy had gone back to concentrating on his shot and missed my comment about always paying for it, especially with a woman like the one that had turned Jimmy in. Jimmy paid dearly for her and I doubted she'd been worth it. The chick could barely move most of the time since she remained zipped out of her mind twenty-four/seven. It was hard to believe she became a sexual gymnast when her clothes came off.

"I was just wondering... I'd forgotten her name." I

didn't feel like repeating the joke and wanted Jimmy to hurry up with his test. Normally I'd have been more frustrated. Dope addicts that chose to converse while working up a shot severely irritated me. But then again, most of them couldn't multitask like Jimmy, so I decided it better to propel the conversation forward in a more positive direction rather than protest.

"Laurie." Jimmy ripped a tiny ball of cotton from the filter of one of D's Newports and dropped it in the brown liquid. "That bitch. She'd bang five guys a night and sometimes still be short for a fifty bag. That was mostly on account of her old man. Adrian would pimp her out and spend all the money she'd sweated for on his own fix."

"Real winners you were running around with," I said under my breath.

Jimmy didn't hear me. He went on, "I'm gonna find that bitch one of these days. I'm going to shoot to kill too. I'm going to fire like several times. I'm gonna reload and shit. I'm going to empty a clip into that bitch ass."

"Two questions," Paul said from the bed where he sat up next to D who couldn't find anything on the tube. "One. When you say bitch are you talking about Adam or Lauren? I mean they're both kind of bitches when you look at it a certain way."

"I said I was going to kill both of them."

He hadn't actually said that, and I'm glad Paul didn't point this out as he was already doing a swell job irritating Jimmy O'Hearn, a man not known for patience. All Jimmy had talked of was shooting Laurie.

Paul leaned against the headboard. "You could have

been a little more precise with your words."

Paul and Jimmy had never met until tonight. My ex-con, junkie guru looked at me and nodded at Paul. "Where did you find this goddamn comedian?" Jimmy was not impressed with my new friend. He hated smartasses and I never understood how he could stand me.

D began laughing at the bickering between these white boys. "Y'all fucked up."

"Everybody keep your composure," I said. "Paul's probably just as scared of you as you are him, Jimmy?"

Jimmy drew the brown liquid through the cotton into the syringe until the heroin reached thirty C.C.s. "I'm not scared of that pansy."

Paul rose from the bed and began pacing again. "Pansy? I shot a man in the face today. What have you done with your life besides a bang up job as a drug addict?"

Jimmy wasn't listening anymore. It was good thing too, because I'm pretty sure he had killed a drug dealer who'd sold a good friend of ours a hot shot on the thin suspicion that the guy was an informant. Paul's words would've been a cause of great contention and the last thing I wanted to do today was see more violence or have to break up a fight between friends. I wanted my money, a shower, and whatever rest I could get considering the nightmares I'd have to ward off.

The needle had pierced Jimmy's flesh. As blood drew up into the syringe, he quickly brought the plunger down. His eyes rolled into the back of his head for a few seconds before the lids closed then a shiver ran from his feet to his groin causing him to shake a bit before untying the belt around his bicep and removing the needle from his forearm. "That shit's good."

Paul forgot his anger and approached the now heavily stoned felon. I stood next to my business partner, both of us staring down at the satisfied hophead like scientists observing a mutating specimen.

"Really fucking good." Jimmy shivered again for a moment then crossed his arms and rested his head on the window-side table.

The bundles netted us just over two grand after subtracting the start-up cash Paul and I had put out and what we'd have to pay Parrant. I'd cut the shit out of the dope but Jimmy still swore by the heroin's high. I'd thrown him two hundred dollars in the motel parking lot and he'd immediately sprinted over to D's car, tapping on the window to beg to buy.

I sat in the passenger side of Jimmy's Trans Am. He'd offered us a ride back over the bridge when D announced we should travel separately after the killings and all. As the new kingpin collected his new product, locked it in his suitcase along with his scales and gun, he'd asked where I'd found such fire dope.

I'd refused to go into detail. I'd told him, "Far up north. Farther than you and yours would want to travel with that much heroin."

"Detroit?" D had asked.

I could see the rusty wheels turning in D's sinister and blighted brain. He wanted to cut out the middle man and steal my connect.

"Was it Cleveland?" D grinned, telling himself he must be getting warmer since I'd grown more silent with each guess as he rattled off: Dayton, Chicago, Gary.

"Let me worry about where I get it." I winked at D. He'd stopped smiling. Maybe that was why he told me and Paul to find our own ride back to civilization even though he swore the measure to be solely precautionary.

"He was punishing us for not telling him about Roach and Cinci," I said to Paul from the front seat of Jimmy's Trans Am without turning to look at him. I couldn't divorce my eyes from the smooth, crisp stack of fifties stacked in the brown paper bag in the floorboard.

The night before I was to pay Officer Jody Parrant his first week's tribute, I lay on my futon with the stack of money for which I'd shed blood and forever watered down my conscience. The thought of handing this money over to the dirty pig made me sick to my stomach, having to risk my life and freedom again Monday morning on which I'd agreed to meet Roach in Covington to make another buy. The uncertainty of how long Paul and I would be Parrant's whores only added to the overall sense of hopelessness that had robbed me of sleep, along with the post-acute opiate withdrawal which, thanks to the Suboxone, no longer included uncontrollable perspiration and chronic shitting. The detox still kept my short term memory depleted and my brain fixated on lousy memories and unrelenting self-hatred.

I crossed the cold hardwood floor of my studio apartment to the dresser where I kept my bills in two stacks, personal utilities, and those associated with the bookstore.

I owed Louisville Gas & Electric three hundred and

fifty dollars. The sheet of paper I studied was what poor Louisvillian's had nicknamed a brown bill because rather than green, the company's signature color, the numbers and details in shut-off notices were all typed in brown boxes and rectangles, the color of the shit the monopoly always stuck to us each year when their rates hiked five to ten percent.

The rent, $3200, always due at the third, had become the real issue, I'd fallen a month behind and had paid my landlord a quarter of what I owed him. The next month's payment was only a week away. He was getting impatient though and if I didn't get consistent with my payments soon, I feared walking into work to find an eviction notice taped to the glass of Twice Told Books' front door.

I picked up my cell phone several times and scrolled through my contacts, highlighting Luther Longmire's name and number. I never dialed him, knowing I'd need a little more leverage to get him to side with me over Parrant.

Parrant disappearing would be preferable.

If the cop was no longer a factor, I could easily turn a situation full of liabilities into one lush with assets. I could present Longmire with my Cincinnati connect, offer him cheap, pure dope that he could then rely on for distribution, cornering a lead investor's percentage of the Southeastern heroin trade as he had methamphetamine, cocaine, and marijuana. Only this time not as many people would have to die for him to secure his source.

At least that's what I told myself then.

I had less than twenty-four hours to figure out a

way to screw Parrant out of our coerced arrangement. Then I could worry about getting into business with the billionaire.

Sitting at a bench in Tyler Park, a valley of fountains, foot paths and tennis courts bathed in bright moonlight on the border of Germantown and the Highlands, Jimmy O'Hearn had agreed to hold court with me and Paul. Upon hearing that Parrant had us over the barrel, Jimmy revealed that Parrant had been the one to place the cuffs on Jimmy the night the narcs busted in swinging extendable batons and twelve-gauges. "Bastard laid a beating on me then threatened to tell everyone in jail I was a rat if my lawyer came after him for police brutality." Jimmy then, after a long swig from his silver flask, told us all about Detective Sergeant Mad Dog Mike Milligan, the dirtiest narcotics officer in the city. For a price, he'd allow certain dealers to operate as long as they kept their feuding and inner organizational violence to a minimum. He'd also assist his favorite kingpins, tipping them off to any information fellow narcotics dicks had gathered along with imminent raids and busts.

"He always says that crime can be contained," Jimmy had told us. "If you're willing to make the right sacrifices."

"How do you know all this about him?" Paul asked.

"He offered to make the evidence in my case disappear if I could give him one piece of dirt on Parrant. Apparently when Parrant still worked narcotics, he and another officer were on a stakeout and wound up chasing a suspect on foot. Both the suspect and the other cop were killed. Since, at the time, Mad Dog had been Parrant's superior, he kept track of the loose canons on his crew. He'd spied Parrant in the locker room taping a drop piece to his ankle. Turned out to be the same kind of gun that killed Parrant's partner that night. Parrant swore that the suspect had shot his partner and then he'd unloaded on the fifteen-year old gangbanger out of self-defense."

"Why would Parrant have killed his partner?" I asked.

"IAD were investigating the partner and I suppose Parrant didn't want to take the chance that the cop would divulge the unit's sordid history and get them all fired and sent to LaGrange."

"And Mad Dog did not approve of this decision?" Paul said.

"The dead cop was Mad Dog's nephew. And I also got the impression Mad Dog didn't appreciate his inferior making such an executive decision without consulting the head of the narcos," Jimmy said.

"And I suppose you had no real information that would help this detective?" I asked.

"If I had that Parrant would have been the one to go to jail." Jimmy killed the mixed vodka and tucked the flask in the back pocket of his well-worn Levi's. "But unfortunately, alleged police brutality wasn't enough to even cut a chink in Parrant's armor. Plus, Mad Dog knew if we were gonna come at Parrant, we had to be sure, and be ready to act. I got the feeling if Mad Dog makes the case, he may be planting his own drop gun the night he shows up to bust Parrant."

"So he could help us?" Paul clapped his hands together like a churchman filled with Holy Spirit, ready to stomp his feet down the pews and praise Jesus.

"I can set up a meet with him," Jimmy said.

"Then we're wasting time." I slid Jimmy's cell phone down the bench and tapped on the exterior.

The following night, at just past eleven, Paul and I were to meet Parrant at the Dew Drop Inn on Story Avenue, perhaps the roughest honky-tonk north of Dixie Highway. Jimmy had gotten hold of Detective Mad Dog and told him that if he really wanted to nail Officer Parrant, he might want to drop in at the Dew Drop around ten p.m. "Get there early so me and my associates can fill you in," Jimmy had slurred his words into his cell phone, tired of faking sobriety for the past half hour while he called the Portland Precinct and left messages with three different detectives to have their sergeant call back post haste, that Jimmy had information Mad Dog would not want delayed in delivery.

Mad Dog had called him back within the hour.

In their glory years of speed-induced hysteria and maddening, borderline punk rock antics, great country outlaw singers such as Waylon Jennings and Tompall Glaser had taken the stage at the Dew Drop. The hardcore troubadours often threatened, sometimes even assaulted crowd members who got too drunk to stay on their side of the chicken wire that separated the pickers from the ballroom chaos that left the dance floor sticky with blood and beer at the end of the night.

I'd even been part of the bar's forever undocumented history. The story was now one of the more infamous among ex-Dew Drop regulars. One fine evening at the Dew Drop, I'd knocked a big hillbilly singer unconscious. The guy had ripped me off on a coke deal in the men's room earlier in the night and had disappeared until he took the stage.

I'd then taken his place at the mic to sing some more of his band's poor Lynyrd Skynyrd covers. Apparently the band didn't care too much for him either since they all grinned at me and kept playing.

The owners had long ago done away with the chicken wire since the place had calmed down with the retirements and deaths of Nashville's wildest outlaws. They hadn't planned on me storming the stage and publicly striking the halfwit poser so hard that he dropped his Telecaster, spun one hundred and eighty degrees then fell to the floor shaking. A friend in the crowd motioned for my attention and whispered between numbers that the singer had had a seizure but would survive the incident. I doubted he'd ever try to pass off baking powder as Columbian bam bam to a stranger again. After a song or two, I'd fled the scene before the police showed. I hadn't returned until tonight.

"So you get Parrant talking his shit on this..." Jimmy tucked the small rectangular Radio Shack tape recorder into the breast pocket of my wrinkled dress shirt. "Then mosey into the parking lot and hand it over to Detective Mad Dog. He can probably get IAD on the phone and have this Parrant prick hemmed up before the pig even finishes his last drink."

"Did you hint that maybe IAD should already have been notified?" Paul asked.

We were all slumped in a corner booth. I'd pulled the brim of my mesh hat low. Paul's fedora showed his eyes. Jimmy had pulled his long blonde strands back in a ponytail, Wayfarer sunglasses his only disguise.

We looked ridiculous.

"Who the hell wears sunglasses at night?" I said to Jimmy. "First of all it's a douchebag move. Secondly, it'll just draw more attention."

"I'm going to be in the passenger bucket of Milligan's cruiser peaking through the windows with binoculars." Jimmy ignored my inquiry. "Your precious little Parrant will never have to see me. And I highly doubt Milligan wants IAD anywhere near this one. He wants to be the one to make the collar, or to 'attempt to' and that way he has every excuse to shoot Parrant while the scum sucker's making a run for his car, his house, his passport."

"He's just going to kill another cop and hope that this little recording and a throwdown gun will be enough to absolve him of any punitive measures on the part of the LMPD?" I asked.

"No." Jimmy laughed at my inability to keep up with the plan. "The proof is for Milligan. He wants to be sure that Parrant is behaving recklessly. He'd like some proof too, in case someone like Longmire, someone high-up in the game, wants to know why the dirtbag was put under. But Mad Dog will not implicate HIMSELF in the shooting. No, I'd say he's gonna set someone up, make it look like Parrant had a partner in crime, a real felon. He'll make it look like, out of fear of betrayal, this fictional partner in crime flipped out and got rid of Parrant, probably figuring Parrant had the same move in mind."

"How do we know this scapegoat is fictional?" Paul said. "What if Milligan takes out one of us so the cops have a suspect, the best kind too, a dead one who can't tell his side of the story?"

"Or what if he takes out all of us?" I asked.

None of us said anything. We all knew, from a business standpoint, getting rid of one or all of us and blaming the death of Parrant on betrayal within his ragtag outfit of grand larcenists certainly tied up any loose ends.

"I don't think that's like Mad Dog," Jimmy finally said. "He may be dirty but he strikes me as a man who still has a code. I don't think he wants to take out anyone who doesn't deserve it."

"I hate to be the one to say it." Paul took a drink of his Guinness. "But can any of us really say that we don't deserve it at this point?"

"Speak for yourselves." Jimmy laughed as if Paul's idea was ludicrous.

I glanced at my watch. The time was quarter past eight. I had two hours to find Milligan a scapegoat that better served his survival instinct and financial future.

I was certainly glad that Roach had called this morning and informed me of his visit from D.

"How'd he find out you were my man in Cincinnati?" I asked Roach on the phone that afternoon, before I darkened the door of the Dew Drop for the first time in half a decade. I'd just finished weighing the dope I'd bought in Cincinnati that morning.

"He followed you up here this morning," Roach spoke slowly and monotone. "And before we go any further, I thought I warned you to watch your goddamn rear-view for any tales. This nigga could have been FBI, DEA, CPD, any number of police."

"I've never seen an undercover cop look that convincing," I said of D. "First of all, he must have been fairly decent at tailing..."

"... or you fairly bad at throwing tails which would be my bet."

"And his ghettomobile along with his urban enthusiastic sense of fashion would not have set off any alarms in my head that screamed 'COP'."

"All that's fine and good." Roach coughed heavily into the receiver. He'd probably just finished clogging a few more arteries with the day's third plate of short ribs. "But we got more to cover than just your inability to protect our asses and your lack of subtlety."

"What's the problem, Roach? I'm late to a meeting."

"D offered me a slightly better deal. Said he'd add ten percent a gram."

"Oh, he went that high. Always knew D to be a big spender."

"I told him he had himself a deal but also said I was out of product, had to wait for my next visit from Chicago. Buys you a day or two to figure out if you want to meet his price."

"Did you tell him that you're out of product because of me and Paul?"

"In fact I did. Figured that might work into whatever plan you two goofy motherfuckers might concoct to keep the little snake's ass from coiling around your ankles and trying to slow you down again."

"I always knew you had a soft spot for me, Roach."

"It ain't that. I just know you the smarter one and will stay a customer for longer. Call it VIP treatment."

"What about the day you meet a customer you foresee has a longer shelf life than moi?"

Roach remained quiet a moment, laughed, then said, "I guess you better hope I'm in an altruistic mood and give you a call warning you to pack your bags. But let's worry about that day when it comes. For now, you my dawg."

While Jimmy and I waited for Milligan, I called D and told him I had his new batch and that, due to my imminent engagement with my lovely girlfriend Irina (a lie I will always wish had been true), I had to get out of the game.

"You're gonna let that fire dope go for what?" Like the simpleton he proved to be later that night, D never spoke in code when speaking of drugs on cell phones the police could easily have tapped.

"Well, I bought the car for way less than Blue Book." At least if they had me on a wire, I wasn't the one caught talking blatantly about illicit narcotics. "I'd like to make some of my money back, so... let's say three grand."

"Nigga, you crazy. Is the shit all stepped on? Will my junkies even get high?"

"Don't worry," I told him, winking at Jimmy across the table at our booth in the Dew Drop. "Our tester's here and he's fiending."

Mad Dog Milligan's appearance would never have given away his nickname, nor would the manner in which he carried himself. The man dressed like a coolheaded

Blackwater contract killer working out of the middle east—shaved head, black sweatshirt with matching dungarees, and dark brown Timberline work boots. He did not exude madness of any kind, nor did he have the composure or demeanor of a wild dog. Then again, I'd never seen him when tempers ran high.

His age could have been anywhere between forty-five and seventy. Any more specific a guess was deemed impossible by the hard body and young man's gait. He scooted into the booth, pushing Jimmy toward the end of the bench and, without awaiting invitation or permission, finishing Paul's bourbon in one brief pull. Paul walked over from the bathroom just in time to witness this, but taking one look at Mad Dog, didn't say a word. Paul sat next to me, still quiet, tapping on the table top in the fashion of all panicked men who'd ever loved playing drums.

"For the sake of brevity, let's skip over everything about your problem and the players involved that I already know," Mad Dog spoke to me directly. I suppose Jimmy had told him I was the brains behind our crew, or the man with the plan or whatever. With my artistic and slightly collegial attire, slacks, a pressed shirt, and a stainless denim coat, I must have looked far less like a dope pusher than a hipster English professor loved by every swooning co-ed. "So this eternal pain in my ass Parrant, without proper counsel of course, is shaking you fellows down. Jimmy here tells me that you're informed of my history with the little swine. Now I can't prove it in a court of law, but I know the cocksucker killed my nephew like I know every sentence in the Miranda reading. You got cash money here that you're supposed to pay Parrant, correct?"

I explained how Paul and I didn't exactly work for Parrant of our own volition.

"So he's got something on you?" Mad Dog asked before tapping a passing waitress on the hip and ordering a bourbon on the rocks. He stared at the young girl's rump as she walked toward the bar to retrieve his order, saying loud enough for her to ear, "That's outstanding."

"He has a big something on us," Paul spoke for the first time since we'd begun our dialogue with the sergeant.

"And whatever might that be?" Mad Dog turned his attention back from the waitress's ass to his fellow artists of larceny.

"It might be better if you didn't know," I told the older cop.

"Boys, boys, boys." Mad Dog laughed. "Don't you trust your boy Jimmy? Did he not tell you that all I'm concerned with here tonight is nailing and hopefully removing Parrant from this earth. If you're worried I'm going to drag you in for whatever you did to piss him off, you're on crack. In fact..."

Mad Dog removed the gold badge he had clipped to his belt and placed it on the table between him and me. "Now that that's on the table, why don't you tell me what happened?"

I told the story of how I'd killed Parrant's nephew by accident with a dictionary and how Paul and I had dumped the body in the Ohio.

Mad Dog went hysterical with laughter, laughed so

hard he had to stand for a moment to lean over, slap his knees, and catch his breath.

"And you didn't know his uncle was a cop."

"All we knew was that the kid, God rest his irksome soul, was a complete pain in our asses. Kind of like you feel about his hopefully soon-to-be late uncle" I considered ordering a drink myself at this point, but thought my mind would serve me better free of any more outside influences than Parrant, Milligan, and Jimmy.

Finally, I told Mad Dog about my connect in Cincinnati and the disconcerting conversation I'd had with Roach earlier concerning D's plan to cut me out. Mad Dog snapped his fingers. "There's the silver lining, my boys. Now, tell me one of you have invited D to our little sit-down tonight."

"Why?" Jimmy asked.

"I'm so damned far ahead of you, it isn't even funny," I said to Mad Dog then turned to Jimmy. "Remember when we were talking about the idea of a throwdown or drop gun? I already texted D."

"This D sounds like the perfect candidate for a drop gun," Jimmy agreed.

"You didn't think to inform me of this development?" Paul asked.

"What?" I finished my Diet Coke. "I gotta tell you every time I have a bowel movement. It was a good move. Everyone agrees."

At that moment Parrant entered the bar in street clothes, a Carhartt work coat over a black dress shirt and white wash jeans. He actually wore a cowboy hat and had tucked the bottoms of his atrocious Wrangler's into his cowboy boots. I fully expected him to start line dancing to a Garth Brooks song any second in sync with the rest of the morons on the dance floor.

"Seems like a good enough candidate to me." Mad Dog jerked his head in Parrant's direction. "Two birds. One stone. No more D trying to cut you out. No more Parrant trying to shake you down."

"He's gonna want to know what you're doing here?" Jimmy finished his beer.

"Added security," Mad Dog said.

Parrant didn't want to make the exchange anywhere near the bar, especially with Mad Dog watching our backs. He had better leverage in a less public spot. "How'd you idiots even hook up with this Civil War artifact?" he asked.

"I might ask you why you're negotiating shakedowns without notifying your superiors on either side of the law first." Mad Dog finished his Scotch and water. He'd yet to look up at the one cop still on the force he likely held in most contempt.

I texted D that we'd be meeting by the river, where Market Street came to a dead end. I texted him also that I couldn't talk and if he didn't want the deal of a lifetime not to show. On the other hand, if he did want to make a fortune off two dorky, scared, and stupid white boys, to be there in fifteen minutes.

"I just find it odd that the cop I hate most in the entire department is sitting with you three dipshits when I walk in for my first pickup." Parrant pressed a button on the tiny contraption on his key ring. The lights flashed as the horn sounded on a Jeep Grand Cherokee to Parrant's left, a few spaces down so I couldn't make out much through the tinted windows, although I swore I could see the silhouette of someone in the passenger seat.

13

PARRANT DROVE HIMSELF while us men who wished the spineless philistine death and damnation took Mad Dog's Lincoln Town Car. We left the dope and cash in his Pontiac since we weren't going to be handing any of it over tonight, come death or glory. The hesitation to partake in more carnage was painted in rouge and sweat all over Paul's face. But he kept his mouth shut. Apparently he accepted that the only business transaction going down tonight would be multiple homicide.

"Now you're sure you saw someone in Parrant's Jeep." Mad Dog drew a small revolver from a clip on holster around his ankle and unrolled the coil to check the load. The old cop rode shotgun while Jimmy drove, a felon psyched to get his hands on the wheel of a cop's car even though the Lincoln wasn't official LMPD property.

"Breaking the law," Jimmy sang.

"Who in the car is packing?" Mad Dog asked.

"Packing?" Paul said. "Like cigarettes? Chewing tobacco? What the hell are you talking about?"

"Oh shit." Jimmy slapped the empty middle cushion between me and Paul in the backseat. "Paul's in the dark."

"No." Paul shook his head. "The plan's changed and Mad Dog's got a gun. Jon filled me in already."

"This is a good thing, Paul." Mad Dog cleared his throat as he slid the revolver back into his ankle holster.

"A necessary thing. We're going to rid the earth of two scumbags who're doing no one in their families or society any good whatsoever. We're also saving you little shits possible death or jail time. If there's someone else riding with Parrant that can only mean one thing: a setup. He's thinking the same thing we are. We just better hope our plan's better than his"

"And what's this sudden surge of conscience?" Jimmy asked Paul. "You were fine with taking out Parrant."

"I was fine with allowing Parrant and the distinguished Mr. Mad Dog here to settle among themselves."

"First of all, you little punk," Mad Dog eyed Paul through the rear-view with enough disdain to traumatize a prepubescent. "It's detective, not mister, unless of course you happen to be my daughter or grandson, then it's Papa which is exactly what I'm going to make you call me when I shove my revolver up your ass the next time you speak to me in that insolent tone. I'm the one saving your ass and if you have to witness a few gun thugs dying in the same fashion they lived, stomach it. You can use the extra thousands we're able to keep to dry your eyes later. Now you," Mad Dog glanced at me then pointed at the glove box, "open it."

Inside the glove compartment the tiny bulb bounced light off of a small revolver.

"Well, don't just give that fire barker come-hither looks," Mad Dog yelled. "Flirting time's over. Pick the gun up and stuff it in the pocket of your coat."

I looked at Paul, then Jimmy.

"Why me?" I retrieved the gun and stared at the cold steel in my palms for a moment.

"You're the queerest looking of all of us." Mad Dog hung a left on Market. "They ain't likely to search you if it comes to that. I know Jimmy's packing and despite his demeanor tonight, Paul just looks mean. As a matter of fact..." Mad Dog knelt to reach to the small of his back and drew a tiny automatic that he tossed back to Paul without looking. The gun bounced back and forth between Paul's palms like a hot potato before he finally got a grip. "When they pull on us and ask for the dough, the three of us—me, Paul and Jimmy—all toss our weapons. If they ask about you, we'll laugh out loud, make you for the brains, maybe even bust your balls a little."

"What if they search me anyway?" I asked. The threads of Mad Dog's plan had already loosened in my mind.

"You'll have to act quick." Mad Dog rolled down the window to let in the cool breeze from the river as we neared. "Start the show early."

"The show?" I had just begun to realize that either way things went down, I was going to be the first one to open fire. "While Paul's pretending to get the product out of the trunk I kill both of them." I could hear the resignation in my own voice.

"It's not like this is your first rodeo, kid." Mad Dog pulled into the same lot where Paul and I had brought Carter's body.

When we exited the car by the riverbank, the small square parking lot was empty.

"Don't make sense," Jimmy said. "Parrant left before us. He should be here by now.

"Yeah." Mad Dog shook his head, weary and suspicious. "This is a setup. Any minute..."

From our left, from amongst the dark of a small cove of trees, a greasy, dwarfish fellow in leather pants and a biker jacket emerged with a sawed-off double-barrel trained on us. I heard a rustling to my right and turned to see Parrant leaning against a sagging abandoned shed. He held leveled on me and my new, temporary crew, a massive Desert Eagle 50 caliber hand cannon. Seemed like overkill to me. Me and Jimmy had fired one of them at the Knob Creek Gun Range and the pistol sounded like a tank when it went off. Cops on Broadway could probably hear the thing going off from the river where we now waited to die or kill.

Mad Dog put his hands in the air. The rest of us followed suit.

"Good," Parrant said. "Saves me breath. Now drop any firearms you may be carrying on the pavement and kick them over here."

Mad Dog tossed his ankle piece, the clatter in chorus with sounds made by the pistols Jimmy and Paul dropped.

"What about Professor Dick Cheese?" Mad Dog tilted the barrel of the hand cannon my way.

Mad Dog laughed. Paul and Jimmy awkwardly joined the detective, manifesting their collective amusement at the idea of me with a gun. "This kid with a piece?" Mad Dog asked. "He'd blow his own pecker off. But one of you two are welcome to come over and feel him up if that's what gets your meat to loaf."

"Your a shifty one, Milligan. I'll just trust my 50 cal here to spread you all to hell, anyone makes any fast moves. Plus, I believe you. That pansy would mistake a gun for his dildo and end up with a .45 round in his colon."

Swarthy and Parrant shared a hearty chortle for a few seconds, then it was back to business. For a moment, both our adversaries and the men on my side all laughed at me together. Even though I knew it was part of Mad Dog's ruse to make jest over yours truly, having to shut up while six bad men took their time laughing at you is always an ego deflation.

"You keep these three occupied. Whoever has the keys to the trunk, come with me and give me my goddamn money."

Jimmy and Parrant crossed the lot to the Lincoln, leaving the rest of us to Swarthy's mercy, or, hopefully, stupidity.

There we stood, Paul emasculated and disarmed, me, the alleged effeminate brains of our organization, obviously, to these men at least, without the cunning or the ruthlessness needed for murder. They must have thought Paul killed Carter and took care of the cleanup while I stood back, my hands clean of river silt or blood.

I began laughing maniacally.

"What's funny?" Swarthy asked.

"You're the one that's so fond of knives, right," I said to Swarthy. "Parrant's warned us about you, threatened us with your blade before. Yet you have to use a gun to kill a harmless gnat like me. I'll die knowing that Parrant's words were lies and that you're a dickless coward."

"Shut up." Swarthy stepped closer, lowering the

sawed-off to shoot from his hip.

"I bet I could kick your fucking dick in the dirt, you greasy after-birth looking son of a bitch. I may look fancy and educated and everything lowbrow goons like you disdain, but I ain't never lost a fight. Shit, you can even use your knife if you want."

"Jon..." Paul placed a hand on my shoulder.

"Get your goddamn hands off of me." I shot a murderous glance Paul's way then turned my eyes back to the knife wielder. "Now are you gonna stand there all day behind the safety of those barrels or are you gonna come at me?"

As soon as Swarthy lowered the shotgun, I began to remove my coat, as if in preparation for a street fight. Wrapping the jacket neatly around my forearm, I got my hand on the revolver's grip in the coat pocket. I could hear footsteps behind me, Parrant distracted, probably just now discovering the crumpled paper bag we had brought empty.

"What the hell is this?" I heard Parrant say behind me.

"Hey, Parrant," Swarthy obviously hadn't heard his partner's discontented commentary and kept his shotgun lowered. "Watch me beat the shit out of Encyclopedia Brown here."

It was now or never. Despite my proclivity for many things academic, I'd grown up around hillbillies in Perry County, Kentucky, been shooting guns since I could figure out how to use my fingers properly. I'd escaped Hazard when I was seventeen and never looked back. But some skills stick with you, no matter how lousy the memories.

I fired three times through the denim of my coat, each chest shots. While Swarthy staggered and dropped to his knees, I turned to face Parrant. Jimmy clawed at the cop's wrists, struggling for the gun. Parrant headbutted Jimmy. I took two giant strides forward and shot the bent cop in the face before he could draw a bead on me with his hand cannon.

The near decapitated corpse landed flat on its back. Behind me I heard gagging and choking. I turned to see Swarthy crawling, placing his hands on the shotgun he'd dropped when I'd fired on him. In one quick flash of movement, Mad Dog grabbed the smoking revolver from my hand, ran over to Swarthy and fired twice into the back of the dying man's head.

Paul, dry heaving against the driver's side of Mad Dog's Town Car, pointed his shaking index finger at the car pulling up from the main road. Bright headlights illuminated the fresh crime scene.

When the car turned slightly to fit into one of the few parking places, I said, "Shit, I completely forgot about D."

14

MAD DOG FLASHED his badge and held the drop piece on D as the gangbanger exited the driver's side of Rig's old Escalade. He put his hands up, stepping far away from the vehicle, yelling that he hadn't done nothing.

"I know you," Mad Dog said. "DeAndre Clemens. I used to take care of your boss. Watched his back, kept him off the radar and out of handcuffs. For a shitbird, he wasn't so bad. In fact, I kind of liked him. You on the other hand, are a real pain in the dick. You'd hurt or kill anyone to get ahead, even when you had it made with Rig. You had it made better than a bench lawyer. You've left more than a few bodies in your rise up the crack corporate ladder. So don't tell me you 'ain't done nothin'. Just last week I watched the coroners zip Raymond Riglett up in a big black body bag. He was also known as Rig, and like I said, it's going to be hard to find a drug dealer I like working with half as much as the late Raymond. You don't think I know you were the one who set him up, DeAndre? Your pockets are a lot thicker now thanks to Rig's untimely demise."

"I didn't have nothing to do with that, man," D said.

"That's not what your homeboy Randall said before he expired at the scene." Mad Dog thumbed the hammer down on the .38 as he stepped closer to D. "That's right, moron. You left a living witness. Too bad he didn't live long enough for us to Grand Jury him. But unlucky for you, I was the one he spilled his guts to, proverbially speaking, and that's enough to leave you fucked, kid."

"Wait." Paul had pulled himself together enough to join us again. "All that killing that day. That was you?"

"You two were there?" Mad Dog leered at Paul and me with the dead eyes of a great white shark. Only a moment of anger flashed across his pupils then he was all business again.

"We were supposed to be meeting Rig so we could unload some of the dope so that we could pay that dead asshole back there." I bit at a hangnail and shrugged. I was getting used to people pointing guns at one another. "Then everyone started killing each other."

"That's right," D crowed. "Everyone started doing some killing."

"What the hell's he laughing about?" Mad Dog asked me.

"He's got guns with our prints on them." Paul kicked the wheel of the Lincoln. "The same ones used to kill Russell... whatever his last name was."

"Russell Smithers. I don't even want to know how you two jerk-offs let that happen." Mad Dog lowered his gun. "Jimmy, call it a hunch, but entertain me a moment and go over and frisk young DeAndre."

While Jimmy ran over and began patting down D, Mad Dog searched D's new Caddy. Paul stepped over to my side and began his latest round of blame and character assassination. "I have a kid. I'm in college getting a Master's. I could have still had a future. But no. If Jon's going to hell so are his friends, right. Misery

105

loves company and all that."

"No one held a gun to your head." I refused to even look at Paul. He was a grown man, older than me, and got off on the game just as much as I did, if not more, considering the closest he'd ever come to committing a crime since his late twenties involved a dime bag of weed, an addie prescription, and marijuana paraphernalia. In his youth, he loved degeneracy, picking fights just to end them with his brawn and evil. He missed the action, the rush of impending violence.

"You're my best friend." Paul shoved me, tears in his eyes. "I can't turn my back on you. But I didn't think you'd lead us here."

"Girls," Mad Dog yelled. He stood in the headlights of the Escalade, his pinkie finger in the trigger guard of the same kind of gun with which D had made Paul shoot Russell. "This look familiar." Jimmy had also discovered the Browning I'd shot Russell with in D's waistband.

"Where's the other one?" I asked.

"In my coat pocket," Mad Dog said. "Idiot had two murder weapons in his glove box."

Behind Mad Dog, D fumed, cursing himself, finally punching out the back passenger window of his SUV.

"Simmer down there, Thug Life." Jimmy stuck the barrel of his Beretta to D's temple. "You're giving yourself away."

"Those are the guns," I reassured Paul, slapping him on the back annoyingly. "At least looks like it." He took a deep breath and shrugged my hand off, but I could see honest relief in his comparatively relaxed features and his deflated pose.

Mad Dog turned to D. "You figured you'd make sure all three of you had blood on your hands. By the way, if you've been carrying this piece around for a week, how did you think anyone could pick up any prints after you put your hands all over the gun?"

D's eyes bulged and then he hung his head, ashamed of his own ignorance.

"No wonder the shelf life of you gangsters is so damn short." Jimmy said. "You all aren't exactly giving Stephen Hawking a run for his money in the intelligence department."

D giggled. "Well, at least I made some men of these two white bitches right here." D nodded at Paul and me, interrupting our stare down.

"Men?" Paul looked at the kingpin. Then he examined the firearms lying on the pavement. He looked at Mad Dog and asked, "How would it play if Parrant had killed D?"

"DeAndre shoots Parrant and the knife wielder but Swarthy gets him with the shotgun before D can make it to the Escalade," Mad Dog said. "That'd play better."

"What y'all talking 'bout?" D edged sideways towards the Escalade's driver's door.

Paul strode over to Swarthy's body, bent down, retrieved the sawed-off and turned to D. "If I'm gonna have blood on my hands, what difference will one more asshole make?"

Then Paul let loose of both barrels and blew DeAndre Clemens all over the side of his tricked out Cadillac.

15

WE'D CROSSED THE river, the sound of sirens behind us, quiet as the still midnight water below. I tossed my shot up denim jacket along with the guns D had on him over the bridge. We left the thirty-eight and the sawed off, both wiped free of our finger prints, at the scene to leave the impression that the three men had killed each other during some sort of falling out.

Mad Dog stopped at a Texaco on Main Street in New Albany and ordered us to the bathroom to wash up and clean the blood off our hands and faces. The bathrooms were located on the side of the building so we didn't have to walk in and be seen blood soaked and pale-faced with shock, looking like Kentucky vampires after a low class feasting. When we'd cleaned off, at least enough to be seen in public, without a discussion in regards to our destination, Mad Dog pulled into the lot of a Waffle House.

He told us we all needed to eat something and have a little talk about our collective and respective futures.

The only other customers were two truckers sitting at the counter grunting over empty plates wearing the same kind of mesh caps I'd left in the trash can at the Texaco bathroom.

We sat at a corner booth, Paul next to me, Jimmy and Mad Dog across. When the big boned waitress who didn't skimp on mascara arrived, we all ordered coffee. Jimmy wasn't hungry, probably due to having shot up a quarter gram of mine and Paul's heroin at the Texaco. Paul ordered toast. Mad Dog and I had the same special, waffles with chocolate chips and cheese covered hash browns.

"I'll be damned," I said as the waitress walked toward the smoking kitchen to put in our order. "Me and Mad Dog got something in common. Those chocolate waffles are almost better than dope."

"Bullshit," Jimmy mumbled.

"Those waffles are the only thing I got in common with you, dumbshit." Mad Dog sipped at his coffee. "You three—that is if Jimmy considers himself part of your crew—are sitting on a goldmine. I took a look at some of your dope that's been hitting the streets. It's the best this town has seen since the late 70s when we were a hub for the southeastern heroin trade. People from Atlanta, Florida and sometimes even Chicago would meet in this smaller city to avoid any setups or heat from the Feds. And the best part is, you guys, minus maybe Jimmy when he hasn't showered for a few days, do not fit the drug dealer profile."

"I knew we were onto something." I patted the back of Mad Dog's hand and thanked him for sharing my brilliant vision.

"You ever touch me again, I'll kill you." Mad Dog pulled his hand out of reach. "You have turned your vision, which should have been executed with the precision of Goya painting one of his masterpieces, into a drunken Jackson Pollock rip-off. Since you've began your business almost ten people have died. I don't know if the boys in Homicide will buy the setup I rigged back by the docks. If I were investigating it, I'd see it as a clear case of Parrant stepping in the dirt and getting too dirty to ever clean up. I made sure to get gunshot residue on each of their hands. That's why I fired a few rounds with their fingers on the triggers. We're probably in the clear. But if you nincompoops don't get your shit together, and I mean quick, you're gonna get yourself so deep into some quicksand that I can't pull you out."

"I gotta ask," Paul said. "At some point Parrant bragged about being on Luther Longmire's payroll. Is Longmire gonna look into this and come after us?"

Mad Dog chuckled for the first time since The Dew Drop Inn.

"Who do you think introduced Parrant to Luther?"

I grinned from ear to ear. "So you work for Luther too?"

"I don't work for anyone but myself. I assist. I assist the LMPD in keeping crime contained to neighborhoods where people don't vote or pay taxes. I assist Luther Longmire in security matters. And when I say security matters, think of that job like this: when you think of security, you may think the word to be synonymous with defense. I believe a good defense is a lethal offense. That's the kind of security I provide for Luther. I used to provide services for our mutual dearly departed friend, Rig, but I suppose I'll have to be updating my resume if I want to keep my income at the same level it's been. That's why I took you boys to breakfast instead of throwing you in the goddamned river. I need a job, but I'm not going to work with some grab-assing idiots. Things are going to have to change if you kids want to become rich and avoid twenty-five year prison sentences or the fate of the men we just dealt with."

"You ended that sentence with a preposition." Paul accepted his small plate of toast as the server dispersed our food. "Other than that, great speech. I agree with all of it. My problem, Mad Dog, is..." Paul waited until the waitress had disappeared behind the swinging kitchen doors. "I don't want anyone else to die because we want to make a lot of money."

"They won't have to." Mad Dog said through a mouth of cheesy hash browns. "Not if you let me advise you."

16

IRONICALLY, LUTHER LONGMIRE'S home, surrounded by ten rolling acres of grazing cows, fenced-in horses, rolling creeks and woodland, had been painted bright yellow. Yellow, the color generally associated with cowardice, in no way applied to the Luther I'd heard stories of since childhood, the south end bred strip club bouncer turned bookie turned vice kingpin of Louisville and the rest of Kentucky. Today, Paul, Jimmy, and I were blessed by Mad Dog to have a meet with the Godfather of the Bluegrass.

I'd dressed to the nines, a blue button-down, an ascot covering my neck, a black suit coat, trousers, and knock-off Italian loafers. Paul dressed up in his own way, unwilling to break his intolerance for polite society, "especially since we're meeting a flagrant criminal" as he'd put it. He didn't look bad though in his leather jacket with a dress shirt beneath and jeans that appeared well washed and ironed. Jimmy had stayed behind to man the store. Despite his rough exterior, he'd worked with me before at Twice Told Books. He was a great salesman and knew the ins and outs of the used book business, what to buy if a customer was selling and how much crap to put up with from a Highlands weirdo before banishment became appropriate.

Mad Dog had taken the driver's seat of his other

personal car, a black Dodge Charger, dressed like a mortician, all black save the white suit shirt. He had done us a favor, selling the heroin Paul and I had brought down from Cincinnati for the late D to Luther for a fair price and only keeping a fifteen percent finder's fee. There was a flip side to the influx of cash: if Luther's tester came back with a negative report, Paul, Jimmy, and I would likely wind up with Carter in the Ohio. So far, we'd heard nothing back, which meant, despite my general ne'er-do-well attitude, I was close to defecating in my nice, smooth slacks. Me and my best friend faced the possibility of never leaving the pretentious suburb of Anchorage alive.

"Now if either of you two dipshits do or say anything to embarrass me, I will not hesitate to shoot you." It was as if Mad Dog were reading my thoughts of ill-fate and mortality.

"In Luther's living room?" Paul asked from the backseat. "I don't think that would go over to well with the big man."

"We'll probably be meeting by the pool." Mad Dog winked at Paul in the rear-view. "That chlorine is great for dissolving at least a few pints of blood."

"Shit." Paul placed his face in his palms. I had been worried about my partner since we'd begun our odyssey through the local underworld. But he'd seemed noticeably less worried since he'd shot D. Perhaps he'd finally crossed over from pseudo-innocent to self-acknowledged bad man.

The killer cop parked the Charger behind the open garage just past the three-story mansion. As he removed the key he stared out the windshield as he finished warning us of the consequences of any untoward behavior. "If you can sell this man on the proposition, on the idea I just handed over to you two, you will make a lot of money and, if you follow mine and Luther's lead, two men who've been in this business decades and aren't under investigation by any law enforcement agency, you might just walk out of the game unscathed."

Mad Dog didn't mention when listing the benefits of Luther's patronage that no one just walks, not from a man like Longmire.

I had to learn that part on my own, the hard way.

The interior of Luther's home had been decorated in polished pine. Beams crisscrossed the tall ceilings, subtracting some of the plantation feel from the place, adding a touch of modernity. Luther exited the kitchen wearing his usual regale, a Stetson, a plaid work shirt and torn jeans. He never dressed like a millionaire and I didn't understand why Mad Dog insisted on us appearing so formal. "It's a sign of respect" was his answer when I brought up the fact that Luther always looked like an out-of-work lumberjack.

"Boys, boys, boys." The six-foot-one, ruddy faced drug lord shook each of our hands. The guy had a grip. I thought he was going to break all five of my fingers when it was my turn to suffer his handshake. Like Mad Dog, Luther had taken great care of himself, making his age difficult to discern by appearance alone. He had small crow's feet at the corners of his eyes, but those were the only signs of aging apparent. He might have been forty-five. He might have been old enough for social security eligibility. One thing was for sure about Luther Longmire though; the man was a survivor. "Milligan here tells me you're the smart one." Luther slapped my right shoulder as hard as he'd shaken my hand. "Then again, I already knew that. How are you doing, Jon?"

"I've had better years." I grinned earnestly at the drug king.

"I didn't know you were street smarts," Luther said.

"I'm working on it." I flashed Mad Dog an incredulous glance, considering the peg or two he'd taken me down the night before, referring to me and my partners as moronic and bull headed. I drew my attention quickly back to the man of the house. "I mean I'm the one who got these squeaky wheels spinning so to speak." I winced at my own cliché, then smiled awkwardly.

"Well, from what I understand, you boys have a hell of a thing going." Luther slapped me on the back. "Plus I wouldn't mind a few more music recommendations." Luther pointed at me and looked over at Mad Dog. "This kid knows more about American music that anyone I ever met. He gave me this album by John Phillips, the main writer for The Mamas and the Papas. I must have listened to that damned thing for two months straight."

Mad Dog smiled politely and said, "That's something," clearly not caring a bit about my musical knowledge or anything other than the business that needed discussing.

"Call me paranoid," Luther said. "But I prefer to have these discussions outside. Let's take this party out to the swimming pool."

Mad Dog beamed. He'd been right about the pool.

115

I hoped he didn't have to fill the chlorine water with our blood.

"To the pool, gents." Mad Dog ushered us out of the foyer.

We sat in beach chairs at a round table a few feet behind the diving board of the oval shaped pool several yards from the house. I noticed that there were no plants or rosebushes or greenery whatsoever surrounding the lounge chairs and pool. Luther had left no place for the Feds to hide microphones to monitor his poolside conversations.

"Before we go any further," Luther said. "We need to put this unfortunate Parrant situation past us. You know how I intend to do that?"

I scowled. "How?"

"Thank the Good Lord I got one less loose canon to worry about." Luther laughed. "You boys done me a favor getting that prick out of my hair. Milligan here told me you was sweating bullets, wondering how I'd react. Parrant didn't seek counsel before going on with his little shakedown operations like the one he was working on you two. He didn't talk to Milligan and he didn't talk to me about it. If he'd gotten jammed up with IAD, that could have effected Mad Dog and me. But Parrant didn't give a shit about the greater good. He just loved the power of pulling people's strings like some hillbilly puppet master."

I was still sighing with relief when Luther finished talking.

Paul had recovered more quickly from the pleasant

revelation that we would not be forced to our knees and shot execution style in the back yard of a house in the neighborhood we both hated most in the city. It would have been a fitting death for two layabouts for an Anchorage swimming pool, a neighborhood mostly made up of assholes, to be the last thing we ever saw.

"So Parrant stays in the past?" Paul asked.

"As long as the police keep saying that the colored boy or the greaser killed Parrant." Luther laughed again.

The papers say Parrant was pressing D and Swarthy—the guy I killed first turned out to be named William Maplethorp, but I liked Swarthy better—for information, going above and beyond the call of duty when an argument broke out, got heated, and guns were brandished.

"That dipshit Parrant is going to get every medal the LMPD has to offer and a hero's funeral to boot," I said. "Man do the police suck, heralding a fart factory like him."

"Makes sense." Mad Dog lifted his glass and held it a few inches from his mouth, waiting to finish speaking to take a drink. "You want to cover up a bad cop, you make a hero out of him. That's a trick the brass has played for years. Parrant was a piece of shit." Mad Dog drained his glass. "Now that we're past that uplifting subject, Jon, why don't you tell Luther about your connection up north and about the mistakes you've made thus far? Then inquire as to how he would handle such matters in the future and ask whether he's interested in helping you, you stumble bumming little bastard."

I saw movement inside the breezeway, a woman in a black dress with a drink in her hand. She had the figure of a 1950s starlet, but the screens obscured her face.

"Your turn to talk, Jon," Paul said.

"After such a wonderful speech..." I buttoned my coat and giggled politely at my own sarcasm. "I don't know where to begin. I mean, Mad Dog, how do I follow such gracefully executed oration?"

Mad Dog kept his eyes on the pool's slowly waving water and shook his head. "You're treading, kid."

"Goddamnit." Luther slapped the plexiglass table top. "Do I really have to start your business presentation for you, kid? No wonder you've gotten yourself into so much trouble. It's all shits and giggles with you. How's that attitude worked so far? From what I understand you have a failing bookstore and you've had about the same amount of success in the dope game." Luther allowed a moment for his harshly spoken truths to sink in. "However, the shit situations you have gotten yourself in, you've found rather clever ways out, and you're pushing the best dope this city has seen in decades. This interests me greatly. You see, children, the only drug market I've yet to corner is heroin, since it's only made a resurgence in Louisville over the past three years. I don't have any connections to a large-scale supplier. You do. My proposition is this, together, we go to Cincinnati, offer your contact a lump sum to introduce us to his wholesaler because I guarantee your boy is buying this fire off someone else. Everything in Cincinnati and further south, heroin wise, comes from Chicago, Detroit, New York or Baltimore. It's that simple."

"You're right," I said. "My guy is still just a glorified middle man. And if we connect with the wholesaler, we'll get a better deal and a larger return on our investment."

"I'm glad you're open to suggestions," Luther said. "We have other business too, almost as pressing. Since that genius Rig's gone there's now a vacuum in the West End drug market. We need to move fast with all this so I can place one of my boys down there to push your product. That way we control all aspects of the business. I can also export the dope to Lexington, Owensboro, Nashville, Memphis, and half a dozen other cities, along with the mountains of Eastern Kentucky where my people come from. That place has never had any good heroin and since the Feds are cutting down on Oxie sales, making all kinds of regulations, the junkies in Harlan and Perry County are having a hell of a time staying well."

"What would our next move be then?" I asked. "And what role would Paul and I play in your organization."

"The next move is setting up a meet with all four of us and your connect," Luther said. "And your role... think of yourself as an ideas man. You know I think you're immensely intelligent. You've gotten out of some hairy situations without so much as a scathe and it was you who first brought that brown fire to town. You and your friends will be paid handsomely and worry not... I will treat you as equals. You will run the heroin portion of my organization. I'll just be taking a fifty percent cut."

"Fifty percent." Paul sat up. "Wait a goddamn minute."

"Paul." I rubbed Paul's right shoulder. "Our cut will still be much larger than what we would make working by ourselves. Am I correct, Mr. Longmire?"

"Call me Luther, son." Longmire smiled sentimentally

as if already trying to play the father I never had. "The fifty percent you pull in will be probably ten times more than you boys would have ever made on your own."

Paul shrugged. As much as he probably found himself loathe to admit it, he knew Longmire was the best option. If you're going to be an outlaw, you might as well run with the best, right?

"Sounds good to us," I said.

We went inside for one last round of drinks, for Luther to make a toast to our new partnership.

That's when I first got a good look at her.

The roan-haired woman in the black dress moved her hips and ass like rotating pistons as she glided into the kitchen and sat a tray of glasses on the massive dinner table around which Luther and his new partners now gathered. In the middle of the circle of glasses was a tall bottle of Pappy Van Winkle, one of the oldest bourbon brands in Kentucky. The bottle probably cost as much as I made at the bookstore in a week. I'd never tasted it, and given the decision I'd made weeks ago, I wouldn't tonight. When the curvaceous, island-skinned woman offered me a glass I told her no thank you.

Luther's jaw dropped. Paul spoke for me.

"Trust me, Luther." Paul accepted his glass from the woman. "Jon's no use to anyone once he starts drinking."

Luther nodded humbly. "Even though it is Pappy Van Winkle, I understand, son. My father was a drunkard. He'd be fine during his stints of sobriety but if he took one drink he was gone. No offense taken. Amara...": Luther got up from his chair and walked over to the woman he'd called Amara and placed a hand tenderly on her bicep. "Could you get Jon whatever he wants, whatever is available in the fridge. The three of us will shoot the shit while you get him liquidated."

"Come with me?" Amara curled her finger toward herself a few times, a lazy, unimpressed light in her dark brown eyes. Her voice was harsh and soft at the same time, like velvet sandpaper.

17

___

IN THE KITCHEN. Amara opened the stainless steel refrigerator door. She stood there with one ankle crossing the other, her head cocked over her shoulder, the light bulbs within shining on her like the spotlights from a Broadway show. "We have Coke, Perrier, Diet Coke..."

"I'll just have Diet Coke," I said. This was the closest we'd been. I stood behind her slightly to the right, appreciating her backside. She had the shoulders of a competitive swimmer and the abdomen of a yoga enthusiast.

"Diet?" She grinned as she placed the white sweaty can on the island and walked over to one of the smooth pine shelves above the sink to retrieve a short glass. "You watching your figure?" She asked, appraising me over her shoulder. She walked back to the fridge with the glass and opened the freezer.

"My figure?" I laughed. "No. It's not that. I just, believe it or not, I like the taste better than regular Coke."

She sat the ice-filled glass down beside the can in front of me. I stood at the edge of one corner of the Island as she leaned against the opposite, less than a foot away from me, lightly bumping her hip against the marble top. "Are you nervous for some reason?"

"Nervous?" I acted surprised at the question even though she had me. The ice grew smaller as I poured my drink, sizzling sounds rising from the mouth of the glass. "Not at all. Why would I be nervous?"

"I was wondering the same thing." She placed her elbows on the marble and her chin in her hands like an inquisitive child waiting for the answer to why the sky is blue or where their dead uncle had gone. "Because up until you entered the house again, you carried yourself with this air of confidence. In fact, you have kind of a swagger when you walk. I bet women love it."

She was killing me.

"I'm the same now as I was outside." I stepped toward the door that led to the living room, but something stopped me from walking away from her, probably the same part of my character that allowed me to jeopardize my business and livelihood over heroin. I turned back to Amara and leaned over the marble, my face only inches from hers. "How'd you know how I'd conducted myself outside? Were you watching me?" I asked, then in the fashion of a wanton game-player like Amara, answered my own question before she could open her mouth.

She nodded "yes."

"I saw you in the breezeway," I said. "Do you snoop around all your boyfriend's business meetings?"

"He's not my boyfriend."

"Are you his maid?"

"There's that cockiness and bravado. You're a bit of an asshole, you know that?" While she'd insulted me, she'd done so with a smile that said something else.

"What are you doing here looking so goddamn good if you're not his woman?"

"I should amend that. He's not exactly my boyfriend.

I'm around just to keep him from being lonely. Luther doesn't do relationships well and he'll tell you that himself. We have an understanding. In fact, we're first cousins."

I opened my mouth to respond, then shut it just as quickly. The cousin comment had left me speechless.

"Don't be so protestant and prudish." She backed away from the island a few inches. "Up until the last eighty or ninety years everyone fucked around with their cousins." A southern drawl escaped her attention, coming out with her words of disdain for my judgments. "There wasn't a damn thing wrong with cousin love."

"They also used to bang little boys in Rome." I decided to play feisty with her and see where that led me.

"Oh, come on." She waved away the apparently inaccurate comparison. "That was hundreds and hundreds of years ago. It's only recently that love between cousins has become so taboo."

She shook her head at me, disappointed that my swagger, that the walking middle finger she thought she'd spied from the breezeway, had turned out so conformist.

Before she could walk away I rushed toward her and placed my hand lightly around her bicep, the same place Luther had touched her. "Wait. Wait. I was just joking. To be honest, and I don't tell a lot of people this, I did it with my cousin twice before her wedding. I still have mixed feelings about the whole thing. Don't walk away mad. That's the last thing I want to come from all this"

She stared at my hand on her arm for a moment. Then her eyes widened as they met mine and she flashed me a smile that exposed an innocence she'd yet to display, like a young girl holding hands with her crush, or finding herself breathless after her first kiss. "I think I have an idea what you want to come from all this. And I'm pretty sure I know now why you were nervous." She placed her hand on mine. "When we first laid eyes on one another, you felt it too."

She pulled me closer breathing deeply into my ear, touching her cheek to mine. Then she walked back into the living room. I heard her tell Luther I'd gone to the bathroom and that I drank Diet.

"Watching his little figure," Luther crowed and the rest joined him.

I noticed something on the island which had been completely cleared when we walked in. I picked up the small piece of paper next to my glass of Diet Coke. Written on the scrap was Amara's name and a phone number.

"God help me," I said.

18

I BORROWED A thousand dollars from Irina this past winter to help pay my rent and power bill. I'd always made enough money at the beginning of the month with online and in-store sales to pay all my expenses and eat well. But, alas, I spent it all on dope in one week. I'd taken no steps to pay Irina back. Every time the store did well for any length of time and I had money to burn, I burnt it on a dirty spoon filled with fire dope imported from Philly or Chicago, through Roach in Cincinnati. I justified my constant delays in repayment, telling myself that she was rich, never had to work a day in her life, and wasn't missing the cash. Now that my head had cleared and Lady Heroin and King Alcohol were no longer my masters, after paying my overdue rent and bills, getting Irina her money back had become a high priority. I didn't want her telling all of her high class friends that I was a bad boyfriend and a deadbeat.

The day after Paul and I joined up with Luther Longmire's crew, I took a thousand dollars of the money made off of D before he died and drove to Middletown, the quiet suburb where Irina and her mother lived in a gorgeous three-story Faux-Château, a highly inflated piece of architecture both in size and price.

I parked on the street, got the flowers Paul had warned me not to bring out of the backseat, tucked the folded manilla envelope full of cash into my back pocket, and approached the front door. I hadn't even made it past the third cobble stepping stone when Irina walked out, her hand on her hip and her face contorted crudely almost to the point of ugliness.

"What the hell are you doing here?" She eyed the flowers with repulsion. "That's funny to me." She stepped into the yard and flicked one of the pedals off the stem. "Something very bad might have happened to a fellow human being who you knew, who I know you saw shortly before his disappearance and not only do you laugh it off, but you refuse to answer my calls for a week."

I dropped the flowers at my feet and reached behind me, coming back with the envelope of cash.

"There's the money I owe you, Irina." I started back toward my car. I could hear a gasp as she thumbed through the cash.

"Hold on a second." Her tone had calmed so I shifted by feet back toward the Faux-Cháteau and Irina running toward me in her cut-off jeans—she loved to show off those tan legs that looked sculpted by the most sex-driven male ever to live—and her Garden work shirt, loose fitting and revealing only slightly the buxom within. "Where did you get this?" She held up the thick, torn envelope, the corners of hundred and fifty dollar bills edging out.

"Business picked up." I adjusted my sunglasses, the sweat brought on by the late afternoon sun causing them to slip down my nose. I had no intention of letting Irina stare me down without some kind of barrier erected.

"And you didn't shoot up the profits?" She shook her head as if still wrapping her brain around the witnessing of a miracle.

"Obviously not." I nodded at the envelope. "Now we're square."

"Have you been sober? You look different."

"A few weeks now, yeah."

"Like no booze or anything? That kind of sober."

"I mean no mind altering substances whatsoever save the antics of my degenerate friends."

She stared at the freshly cut grass for a few moments. I couldn't help but follow her gaze, coveting her feet, her flawless, perfectly fleshy toes and heals. I wanted to suck on the toes and massage her heal. I told myself to kill that line of thinking. Beauty's like a stone within a sling. Find cover or you might get hurt.

"I miss you," she said.

"That would've been nice to know a month or so ago when you walked out."

"When you were a trembling, vicious wreck of a human being?"

"Your leaving didn't help much."

"And I don't know what you're involved in. I mean you show up here with a thousand dollars in cash. Carter's disappeared."

"Keep your voice down," I said. "I'm fine. I'm especially fine considering I had to work like a fucking monk to get you off of my mind."

"I had to worry about myself."

"You're good at that, aren't you?"

"Screw you." She turned and walked away with her

money but—and I'll never forget this image—she stopped to pick up the broken flowers before continuing her trek inside. She stopped again at the cobblestone steps that led to her mother's front door. "Screw you," she said again, turning only briefly to examine the man she'd once called "the love of her life." She was crying. "Screw you" were the last words she said to me for a long, long time.

I called Roach as I promised Luther I would, asking the King of Cincinnati when I could meet with him. I asked him if he'd ever heard of Luther Longmire.

"Sheeet." Roach laughed. "Little Johnny's been shitting in high cotton. What's Luther Longmire want with you? Or me for that matter?"

"I'd just as soon let you two have that conversation."

"I don't like meeting new people. It was a stretch for me to let you bring your skinny, goofy ass butt buddy with you last few times you come up."

"He's my partner and I will not have him ridiculed."

Roach crowed, choking on his own laughter. "God-damn. Jon, you alright. Okay. You bring them white boys to the restaurant on Thursday. We'll talk."

"If it puts you at ease, they want to meet you to try to give you a shitload of money."

"Money's good."

Wednesday evening at about eleven p.m., less than twenty-four hours before the ghetto-legendary introduction of Louisville's biggest cocaine and meth distributor and Cincinnati's most infamous heroin dealer, Amara called

129

me.

"You never used that number." Her voice, that velvet sandpaper, chafed my heart. She'd been the one who'd made it so easy to walk away from Irina the day before.

"The easiest way over one woman is under another," Jimmy had told me long ago. He wasn't always right. But with this particular woman, Amara that is, I think some truth shone through his inebriated misogyny.

"Amara?" The first question that popped into my mind: how did she get my number? Then I remembered Luther had it on his cell and it wouldn't have been hard for her to steal a glance at the contacts list.

"Miss me?" she asked.

"Actually, yes," I said in a slightly smug tone. "I did a bit."

"I can never tell when you're being a smartass or not."

"That means the defense mechanisms I learned as a boy have served me well."

"Luther wants me to watch your store tomorrow. He thinks this habit you've gotten into of closing whenever you feel like it needs to stop. Cops notice stuff like that and you know what their first thought would be?"

"That the store's a front for something."

"There you go, Johnny. You're way smarter than you look."

"Do you know anything about books?"

"No. My entire purpose in life is just to look pretty and sustain the Kentucky stereotype of kissing cousins."

"I'm sorry... I didn't mean to..."

"Gotcha. A little taste of your own sarcastic medicine. Yes. I know about books. Books saved my life growing up in Eastern Kentucky around a bunch of people whose idea of intellectual stimulation included shooting rats in the back shed."

"Sounds like my family. Maybe we're related too."

"You know what I'm talking about. You're from the country, right? Perry County, am I correct?"

"Yes. May we change the subject now?"

"You don't like talking about the hills?"

"About as much as I like discussing male circumcision. Listen, Amara, you got the job. Just make sure not to change a thing about yourself, especially your horrible attitude. In the used book world it's the opposite as usual. The customer is always wrong."

"So that's the reason you've been able to make a living based on your bookstore alone. Pure, unmitigated charm and southern hospitality."

"How about you come in around nine. It'll give me enough time to show you the few things you need to be aware of to run this finely oiled machine."

"If I could get away from here right now, I'd let you spend all night showing me things. We could maybe even work in the oil part too."

She'd left me speechless again.

She showed up wearing her usual black, this time a loose blouse under a leather waistcoat and pants she must have had to jump from a trampoline to fit into. She began sashaying among the shelves, swooning, telling me how much she loved the place, how she'd had a feeling there must be something redeeming about me.

While I showed her the desk and the cash box and the

receipt book, she noticed a single volume I'd been reading next to my laptop, *The Collected Works of William Butler Yeats*. She began flipping through the pages. "Poetry? I would've never guessed, Mr. Ruthless Gangster."

"Real men read poetry." I smiled.

"Read one." She handed me the volume. "Out loud."

"Absolutely not." I stood from where I'd been sitting on the edge of the table. She leaned back in my swivel chair.

"I've never had a man read to me." She lowered her voice. "It's always been a fantasy though. I simply don't know if I could control myself if one ever grew the balls and tried it."

I jerked the book from her hands and flipped through the pages, standing over her as if administering last rites to the dying.

"This one's my favorite," I said to her. "My friend told me that he once read it to a woman trying to get her to fall in love with him."

"Did it work?" The same innocence from the night before returned to Amara's face, her mouth agape. She wanted the poem to have worked on my friend's paramour. She wanted love to have once prevailed. But she knew better.

"I asked him if it did. He said, 'for a little while.'"

Amara turned her face toward the display window. If I'd ever seen someone cry without shedding a tear it was at that moment. "Maybe that's all we can hope for." She rubbed at her eyes and pleaded, "Please read it to me."

The poem was called "When You Are Old." I read every line. She reached for my hand that held the book.

I dropped Yeats to the floor and clasped Amara's soft fingers in mine. She leaned up and savagely kissed me, plundering my heart, and when our lips met I stumbled backwards into one of my shelves, knocking over each of Ed McBain's 87th Precinct novels

I'd believed since our time together in Longmire's kitchen that this woman could get me killed. After feeling her that close, at least at that moment, I didn't care anymore.

19

WE TOOK LUTHER'S black 1975 El Dorado up to Cincinnati on Thursday. I sat in the backseat with Paul and Jimmy while Mad Dog drove. Luther fiddled with the radio from the passenger side, deciding on an old country station playing Merle Haggard. "Anything but some goddamn woman telling me not to drink or cheat, right Jon?" I faked a smile thinking, Luther... I'm sorry. I'm taking your money and now I'm sleeping with your woman. Please never find out. And if you do, please get hit by a dump truck on your way over to kneecap me.

I knew the four of us in the El Dorado weren't the only ones making the trip, that Longmire would have brought a security team. I also knew better than to inquire where they were, which car they were driving, behind or in front of us on I-75. They'd monitor our every move, and some sharpshooter would have a scope on Roach the entire length of the meet. A man like Luther Longmire didn't survive this long without taking certain precautions.

Before Mad Dog opened his mouth about our safety earlier in the day while he packed the trunk of the El Dorado with an Athletic bag full of money and a Mossberg shotgun, the tag-a-long security team had just been a hunch, and, after the two gunfights I'd been in, a strong hope. Once he armed us all, I knew Luther had properly prepared for the worst case scenario.

"Don't look so worried, kid." Mad Dog sneered. It always amused him when me or Paul didn't understand what was going on. As of late, confusion seemed to be our default mode. "We ain't gonna be alone up there. You think Luther Longmire would walk into a big gangbanger's turf without bringing enough men to even the odds."

Paul, Jimmy, and I had met Luther and his main lieutenant at the parking lot of Lowe's off Hurstbourne Lane, a three mile stretch of strip malls, chain restaurants, and car dealerships. While I inhaled my tenth cigarette of the morning and waited for Mad Dog to brief us, I glanced at my watch: ten a.m. We had two and a half hours to hit the mean Cinci streets of Over-the-Rhine.

"We're running dangerously close to tardiness," I told my new employers.

"I didn't know ghetto dope dealer's were sticklers for punctuality." Luther stood at the open passenger door. Today the old man dressed a bit more formal than his usual denim and khaki. He wore a gray blazer over a Polo tee and dress pants. He kept the blazer buttoned to conceal the shoulder rig holstering the massive magnum I'd caught a glimpse of as he'd embraced me earlier, reminding me how much money we were going to make together.

Mad Dog parceled out pistols to me, Paul, and Jimmy. When Mad Dog had seen that Jimmy wasn't packing, the detective asked, "What gives?"

"I didn't want to bring a gun to a meet without permission from you or the big man." Today, Jimmy had gone out of his way to look presentable. Rather than a stained tee and cut off denim shorts, he'd opted for a short sleeve Hawaiian button-down and frayed dark brown corduroys, probably the nicest clothes the recently paroled felon owned. Somehow Jimmy had also managed to mediate his morning shot. The only way I could tell he'd done any dope was when he'd briefly removed his aviator glasses, revealing pupils the size of pin points. "I just figured it best to await further instruction from the big man as far as, you know, how the three of us are to handle ourselves."

"Well, that was a real considerate gesture of respect, unlike the rest of your outfit." Mad Dog popped the trunk and retrieved a nylon gym bag much smaller than that which held the money Luther planned to offer Roach. The bag contained at least five pistols along with a Galil submachine gun missing the clip, I suppose to make room, since the gun's magazine laying off to the side had to be over a foot long. "Damnit, I stuck the spray and prayer in the wrong bag." I'd never heard that term to reference an automatic weapon, but figured it was a cop or military thing since Mad Dog took the Galil, fished out the foot clip and stuck them in the money bag, closing the zipper then motioning to the smaller duffel containing only pistols now.

"Take your pick boys." Mad Dog spat on the pavement, a gesture of all-around frustration. If I hadn't been so terrified of the murderous codger I might have imitated loudly Danny Glover from the Lethal Weapon series, mumbling in the grizzly voice of a blues man, "I'm getting too old for this shit." Instead I quoted Glover just above a whisper and Mad Dog immediately took a street fighter stance, facing me ready to strike with his feet shoulder length apart.

"I just recommended we get on with this shit," I said. "Jesus, Milligan, why don't you take five or something. First your mix up the machine gun, now you're hearing shit. Let's all calm down and have some Cheese-Its or something, ok?"

"Just choose your weapons and we'll be on our way," Mad Dog said.

Jimmy, out of the three of us, by far the most knowledgeable of handguns, picked first, choosing a massive revolver, a Colt Python. I went next picking a gun that had been made famous by one of my favorite series of action movies, James Bond. As I ejected and replaced the clip to make sure the thing was loaded, I asked Mad Dog if I were correct in assuming that in my hands I held a silver Walther PPK.

"Why yes, Agent Double O Dick Suck." Mad Dog reached in the bag and retrieved a police special .38.

Mad Dog shut the trunk and handed Paul the revolver he'd taken from the carry-on.

"Why don't I get to pick?" Paul said.

"Because we're not bringing shotguns and that's the only other piece I'm comfortable with you carrying after seeing you in action by the river." Mad Dog opened Paul's coat to examine the interior and patted one of the inner pockets then jerked the gun from Paul's hand and shoved it barrel first in the leather coat's inner pocket. "That's a .38. The most trustworthy gun a man can carry. It doesn't jam. Its aim is near-perfect. And if you

137

can't hit your target with six shots, you're a dead man anyway. While on the subject..." Mad Dog oscillated his attention from Paul to me and back before saying, "I haven't taken the opportunity to compliment you two on your performance at the docks. You both delivered under extreme duress. And neither of you are used to such situations. Now, don't freak out when I say this..."

"Wait," Paul interrupted. "Why exactly do we need guns for this 'business' meeting?"

Mad Dog rolled his eyes at us "Trust me. It's better to have a gun and not need it than to need a gun and not have it."

20

"IT'S TRULY AN honor." Roach bowed at the sight of Luther Longmire then clasped the old man's liver-spotted hand in his own two massive black paws. "You the man south of Cincinnati."

When we'd walked in, the closed sign had been facing us in the glass of the front door. Roach apparently didn't abide Longmire's attention to detail and consistency. He didn't care what hours he had to close his legitimate business for the sake of his more lucrative endeavors. Of course, Roach owned a considerably smaller operation than Luther and he moved his stash houses every day. If the Cincinnati Police Department tried to keep up with every shady business in Over-the-Rhine they'd have no time to shake down prostitutes or solve murders. Ty, Roach's teenage lieutenant, sat ten feet away at a table working on a basket of curly fries smothered in melted Cheese Whiz.

"I'm a big fan of your work as well." Longmire took a seat at Roach's booth, scooting over for Mad Dog to join him. Longmire looked at me, Paul, and Jimmy and told us he thought it best we three head over to the counter since we might be biased, having a pre-existing business relationship with the impressive and precarious Roach.

There we waited, quiet as tombstones while Longmire delivered his pitch.

Of course there was a problem.

Roach called me over to the table about twenty minutes into the meet. I felt awkward scooting next to Roach, as if I was showing him loyalty rather than Luther, but I also didn't want to squeeze next to Mad Dog who, as he'd said before, would kill me if I ever touched him again.

Roach turned to scowl at me. "Why didn't you tell me these two Foghorn Leghorn motherfuckers want to take food out my mouth?"

"We understand your initial reaction," Longmire said.

"And that's why we're letting slide your disrespectful comments and overall negative attitude toward our business proposition," Mad Dog said. "And I don't see trying to give you a big bag full of hundreds as taking food out of your mouth." Mad Dog kicked the athletic bag, which had been sitting between him and Luther on the checkerboard floor, over to Roach.

"We're willing to pay handsomely for this simple introduction," Luther said. Roach's street talk and urban condescension had drained most of the southern gangster's patience. "All you have to do is call your supplier, vouch for me, Milligan here and whichever ones of these dipshits whose balls have dropped enough to participate in a meet of this importance."

"Ain't gonna be no meet." Roach kicked the bag back toward Mad Dog, the nylon bouncing off of the detective's shin with more force than I'd ever dare exert on the stoic-eyed killer.

Mad Dog exhaled a slow breath then told Roach he

had to use the can.

"And while I'm at it, I'll just lock up this seventy thousand dollars we brought you." Mad Dog lifted the big gym bag and headed for the door.

"Best watch yourself out there old man," Roach shouted. "This ain't the safest neighborhood in Ohio."

Mad Dog laughed and said, "I think I can hold my own," before exiting the chicken joint.

I watched Mad Dog stop at the curb and pop the trunk.

Luther opened his cell phone and offered it to Roach. "Make the call and vouch for us."

Roach shook his head "no." "Besides, there ain't no money in it for me no more."

"That was your choice," Luther said. "But you see, there's a lot more at stake now."

"I'm trembling in my Timberlands, boy." Roach lifted the glass of tea and, as he brought it closer to his lips for a drink, the drink exploded in his hand. On Roach's side of the window adjacent our booth now appeared a quarter size hole. Someone outside had taken a shot and there hadn't even been a sound aside from Roach's glass breaking.

"Bitch ass niggas." Ty rose and drew down, on Paul, neglecting to notice that Jimmy already had his Python trained on the teenager's forehead. Paul rose and drew his Police Special, covering Ty from the side.

"Motherfucker," Roach screamed as he began picking out the shards of glass stuck in his palm.

"If you don't make the call the next one will be a head shot," Luther said then spoke to Ty, still stuck in a pseudo-Mexican standoff with Paul and Jimmy. "Now look here, son. My buddy Cletus who served two tours in Afghanistan is perched on one of them rooftops across the street. If he hears one gunshot from within this building, he is gonna decapitate your boss here with a .30 mag round from the same rifle with which he sniped over a dozen members of the Taliban. Now you want to drop that piece or have your greasy little crown turned into a nappy canoe?"

21

"THEY'RE LEGIT. Sergei," Roach said into the phone. "I'm gonna let you talk to him here in just one second. His new boy Jon's been dealing with me for years and Luther wants the two of them to move up in the world and since this is America, who am I to stand in their way? What? Yeah, I said they was from Louisville. Yes, I said the name Luther." Roach stared down at the table dejectedly. "That's right, Luther Longmire. Yes, that Luther Longmire. Well, I'm sorry, Sergei, I didn't—aight dawg, here he is."

When Luther accepted his cell back he covered the receiver and whispered to Roach, "You should have taken the money. If I could have found this guy without you, there never would have been any meeting between us." Luther, knowing Jimmy was the quickest on the uptake, shot a look at the junkie gunman and snapped a finger in Roach's direction.

"Keep your gun on the kid," Jimmy said to Paul then walked from the counter and sat across Roach at the booth. "Now listen, Tupac. I got this Python filled with hollow points aimed at your balls." Jimmy glanced over at me. "Jon, pull out that James Bond gun and press the barrel to Roach's ribcage."

"After all the shit we been through..." Roach muttered.

"Shut up, Roach." I pressed the barrel deep into his

side. "Like you told me, friendship ain't got nothin' to do with with this game."

Roach leaned over my shoulder and whispered, "What makes you think you cornbread motherfuckers are gonna make it out of OTR alive?"

"We've got ways and means, bro." I thought of the sniper and the team of men who followed us here for protection and, for old time's sake, honestly hoped that Roach, for his own good, didn't do anything dumb.

Luther walked back to the booth from the shadows of the restroom hallway, smiling, satisfied with a business deal closed. He pocketed his cell phone and stood with his thighs touching the edge of our table. "Sergei knows who I am," Luther said. "He was actually quite irritated with you, Roach, for trying to hem up a deal of this magnitude. He thought you'd know better than to refuse us and try to keep your greasy hands on each transaction that passed between Louisville and Chicago."

Roach winced as he plucked another glass shard from his palm. He wouldn't make eye contact with any of us.

"So..." Luther placed his hands on the Formica table top and leaned down, moving closer to Roach. "You screwed up a deal that could have netted you seventy grand for doing nothing more than making a phone call. And now you've probably ruined your Chicago connect and put yourself out of business indefinitely." Luther stood up straight and began back-pedaling toward the front door of the chicken joint. He snapped his fingers and jerked a thumb toward the door. Jimmy and I pushed out of the booth. I grabbed Paul by his free arm, the one he wasn't using to hold the small revolver on a teenager, and then all of us made it for the door.

It was when we got outside that everything went to hell.

Mad Dog leaned against the driver's side of the El Dorado holding his raincoat closed. As we approached he nodded toward the window near the booth where we'd sat. "Better hurry," Mad Dog said. "Your boy's calling in backup."

"Gangsters tend to do that when you put them out of business." Luther ran along the front of the Caddy and gripped the handle of the front passenger side door. Just as he began to pull, the door's window shattered. Luther drew his Magnum and squatted, scanning the blighted avenue for shooters.

A black Trans Am sped onto Short Vine from an alley a block north and screeched to a halt in the middle of the street only a few yards from the El Dorado.

Roach must have had them on standby. Roach's men poured out, each armed with Tech-9s, AR-14s, and brand new police-issue Glocks. The driver, the one who'd taken the shot, drew another bead on Luther. Jimmy, who'd been standing next to our new boss, let off one shot from his Python and the driver descended down the side of the Trans Am, a lush arterial spray flowing from his temple. Jimmy grabbed Luther and shoved him under the cover of the El Dorado roof on the passenger side

Like cowards, Paul and I had ducked and edged ourselves against the driver's side where Mad Dog still stood, bullets flying all around him, sparking off the El Dorado roof and the pavement below.

"Pussies," Mad Dog called us. He opened his overcoat, revealing the Galil we'd seen him transfer from the gun tote to the gym bag earlier. Now I understood why; if things had gone south inside the chicken joint, Mad Dog could have quickly made short work of Roach and Ty. I hoped he could make as effective use of the machine gun with a larger crowd, out here on the street.

Mad Dog removed the safety from the machine gun and racked a round into the chamber. Then, before the rest of us could take account, strode toward the Trans Am, letting off short bursts, the Galil forcing him to plant his feet hard on the street to avoid the gun pushing him backward and throwing off his aim. Luther and the rest of us could not see which of the Trans Am boys had survived.

"Get up," Mad Dog yelled at us, ejecting the clip, dropping it in the outer pocket of his raincoat. "You two look ridiculous. Grown men curled up in the fetal position."

As we stood, Paul said, "I think you have to be laying on your side to really be considered in the fetal position."

"I just saved your pathetic life." Mad Dog hid the gun back beneath his overcoat. "So let's go easy on the wise cracks."

When we appraised the carnage made of the Trans Am, we noticed we now had more company. One white man clad in Kevlar and camouflage appeared from the side door of the parking garage beside Blockbuster across from the chicken joint. A .30 Mag sniper rifle clung to his back, fastened to him by a strap around his chest. He also held a massive handgun, I suppose, just in case he hadn't helped fully clear the scene from the parking lot roof. Another military type, this one stouter, also wearing Kevlar and camo, nudged the body behind the dead driver with his boot heal. "We're good," he said.

"Boys," Luther had yet to holster his Magnum, "meet Cletus." He gestured toward the big boned fellow who'd been checking to make sure everyone in the Trans Am had given up the ghost. "And the man who never misses, Kelly Johnson." Kelly sprinted over to Luther and the two hugged like long estranged kin.

Roach had been waiting for a moment of weakness such as this.

More shooting erupted from behind us. There wasn't enough time for cover. Roach and Ty stood in front of King's Chicken, both firing at us. Neither was a very good shot. They'd jerk the guns forward as they let off rounds as if stabbing someone with the pistols. They were clearly used to close range.

A bullet barely passed me. I could feel the wind of the soaring round against my ear. Simultaneously we lifted the pistols Mad Dog had provided and unloaded them on our aggressors.

Paul stood frozen as we assessed the damage we'd done.

I walked over to Ty, what remained of his head resting on Roach's corpse.

Paul and I together, or one of us, had just killed a teenage boy.

22

WE RENTED TWO rooms at a Ramada Inn in Erlanger, Kentucky about twenty minutes south of Cincinnati. Luther ordered the two ex-military boys, Kelly and Cletus, to return home to the South End of Louisville to be with their families.

"What if those thugs try to come back on you?" Cletus asked in the Ramada parking lot as Luther leaned into the window of the black Jeep Cherokee in which the two killers had traveled to watch over us like angels with arsenals. The sun kissed the river, spreading orange goosebumps across the water as the night introduced herself.

"I don't think there's enough of crew left to cause us any worry." Mad Dog unpacked the gym bag of money and walked over to stand by Luther. Paul and I had just secured two rooms under the name "Kristofferson." The clerk obviously wasn't a country music fan and didn't bat an eye.

Cletus chewed a toothpick. To look at him you'd have never thought that he'd helped commit mass murder just hours ago.

"Plus," Luther said, "I doubt any of these hood rats that worked for Roach have the detection skills of Columbo. We're safe. What's most important is you being ready to move Saturday. First we take Cincinnati, then we take

Chicago." Luther looked over at his newest recruits and said to Paul and me, "You two done good. Now we go up to the room and make our next battle plan. We need to steer clear of Louisville for a few days just in case these geniuses decide to pay you a visit, Jon."

"What about Amara at the bookstore?" I said. "She'll be the one they find if they come looking for me."

"Already took care of that," Luther said. "She's on her way up here. Said she actually made some sales for your lazy ass today."

Paul had gone for drinks. While the other four of us waited in Luther's room, we made small talk. Luther asked questions about the bookstore. Jimmy spent an awfully long time in the rest room, likely getting well, cooking up a shot of the barely-cut dope I'd provided him with for free. He stumbled out of the bathroom, happy as a well-fed Buddha.

Finally Mad Dog looked at me and asked, "Where did a smug little college campus prick like you learn to shoot like that? First that knife throwing weirdo, then Roach and his little bitch boy. I watched and, sorry if this offends your girlfriend Paul, but most of the shots that found purchase were yours, Jon. I'm beginning to think you might just be cut out for this life after all. You don't hesitate and you got a brain for dirty deeds."

We hadn't noticed, but Paul had entered the hotel room, his arms filled with bags of bottles of mixer, gin, vodka, any spirit a drinking man could conjure, all Luther's treat.

"Jon's receiving praise for shooting down a sixteen-year-old boy." Paul tossed the bags on one of the queen size beds. "That's just great."

Mad Dog crossed the room and got in Paul's face before I could respond. "It was them or us. We tried to be civil. Those deaths are on Roach."

"So we had to kill them?" Paul said.

"I don't see how one could look at it any other way." Mad Dog dug his hand in one of the paper sacks and came out with a bottle of Johnny Walker Black. As he removed the cap he continued trying to calm Paul. "We play in the dirt, Paul. It's part of this business. And if you're not willing to get your pretty little hands dirty, you need to walk."

Mad Dog took a swig of the bottle and handed it to Paul, more of an order than an offer. Paul took a drink without wiping the mouth of the bottle, a sign of solidarity, however wavering. Luther walked over and jerked the bottle out of Paul's hand. "Except here's the problem." He took a pull from the Johnny Walker. "You know far too much about my business for us to just let you walk."

Jimmy sat on the other bed. We shared a disconcerting look. We were stuck. We could never walk away from Luther. He wasn't just talking to Paul.

"You said no one else had to die." Paul said to Mad Dog.

"And I wasn't lying." Mad Dog took another pull from the bottle then handed it to Paul who drank hungrily. "No one had to die today. But Roach and his halfwit minions chose so. Luther and I didn't want to do what we did today, just like I'm sure you boys didn't. But a man pulls a gun on you, you ain't got no choice."

"And to quote my favorite saying," Luther said, "'To make Eggs Benedict, you gotta break a few eggs.'"

"I don't think that's the exact saying." Paul took another drink. "I think it's just 'to break a few eggs you have to make an omelette.'"

"I like Eggs Benedict better." Luther shrugged.

Paul's hands had stopped shaking and he smiled for the first time since we left Kentucky. "But I like it. Both the dish and the saying you created. The other one is so played out. I mean it was in Batman and a bunch of other movies I can't think of right now. Original, Luther, really."

"That's my boy," Mad Dog slapped him on the back. "So we're not gonna hear anymore whining from you."

Paul shook his head "no".

"Time to discuss Chicago." Luther reached in the bag of liquor and laid the bottles out on the bed. "Choose your poison, boys."

Paul had been considerate enough to bring a couple of cans of Diet Coke for me, a man after my own heart.

23

LUTHER SAID WE'D lay low at the Erlanger Ramada until the weekend, then we'd travel to Chicago and buy more pure china white heroin than any of us had ever seen in one place. I was hoping to see Amara before it was time for us to leave Luther's room, but he ushered us out around midnight. I finished my Diet Coke then went down to the pool to soak in the Jacuzzi and take measure of the recent changes in my life.

As the jets blew against my back and hips and my fingertips turned to prunes, I listed the things I'd become since I'd accidentally killed that scumbag tweeker.

To be honest, I didn't lose much sleep over the death of Officer Jody Parrant or his swarthy partner in crime or even D. We simply beat them to the double-cross. Someone was going to get screwed and I'm glad it wasn't me or Paul or Jimmy. Actually, since Mad Dog's street smarts and gunplay had helped save my life, I'd begun to grow begrudgingly fond of the bad lieutenant and found joy in his survival as well.

All this introspection and replay of the past month's events, no matter what angle I took, led to a dead teenage boy who would be lucky if the Cincinnati Enquirer mentioned him on page three of the Metro section.

I'd killed Ty in self-defense, I kept telling myself.

I never wanted to kill anyone. But lately, I'd gotten

to a point, sadly, where I didn't much mind.

I had avoided thinking about the kid all night. I'd been blessed with the irksome distraction of Mad Dog and Paul bickering, Luther reassuring us time and time again, from downtown Cincinnati to the Erlanger exit that, all things considered, the meeting was a success. We'd gotten in with Sergei Alvang, the man who ran the Russian mafia's chunk of Chicago. "The beauty part is, boys," Luther had slapped the dashboard, "he already knows he'll make more money than us. He even said he was aware Roach might be a problem and said problem could be settled between me and Roach. So he won't give a shit the jig's taken the big sleep. Also, we didn't have to pay a dime for the intro."

No, I'd thought. We didn't pay in dimes or dollars. We'd paid in blood, and perhaps what was left of our souls.

Finally, like a family of termites slowly digging into my house of memories, images of Ty, dead on Short Vine Street, infested my mind. Half his temple was gone, chunks of brain matter encircling him and Roach. His mouth was open in a manner that might cause one who didn't notice all the holes in him, to think he was still alive and about to say something.

I hung my head over the side of the Jacuzzi and wept.

"What is it?" the familiar voice of velvet sandpaper sounded from my right.

Amara, in a satin robe tied closed, stood at the top of the Jacuzzi steps.

"I can't tell you," I sobbed, shameful bubbles of saliva popping out of my mouth as I tried to speak. She untied her robe underneath of which she wore a tiny black bikini, revealing every curve of which I'd fantasized until this moment. I was sure Luther must be passed out drunk or else she wouldn't have taken the chance coming down here. She would have looked out Luther's motel room window and pretended not to think anything about the newest employee of her cousin/boyfriend/keeper alone, half-naked, immersed in soothing hot water.

She scooted close to me and brought my head to her shoulder, rubbing her hand through my hair.

My survival instinct kicked in and I pulled myself together.

"You have to stop." I knew the right thing to do, the smart thing to do, was to remove her arms from around me, get out of the Jacuzzi and return to my room without another word.

I did not take the intelligent course of action.

In my defense, I did try to verbally prevent the physical contact and emotional intensity between me and Amara from escalating further. "He will kill me for even sitting in this hot tub with you."

"You're a mess." She massaged the back of my neck. "You were crying as if you were at the funeral of a loved one. You're in the midst of some terrible trauma and you shouldn't be alone.

Then she kissed me before I had a chance to speak.

24

THE LONG, WET, inescapable kiss contained a chemistry that Amara alone controlled. I couldn't pull away until she broke contact. Sitting there, a victim of new romance's lustful paralysis, it seemed impossible for me to move past this moment. If I just sat there and kept eye contact with her, part of me believed that maybe we could stay in the hot tub forever as one, holding onto that feeling like a life raft. Then I heard a door open and reality hit me like a wrecking ball.

I ducked down, half my face submerged in the hot tub water. If Luther found us, he'd likely shoot me on sight. He probably wouldn't kill Amara, her being blood, him having some weird protective / romantic draw toward her. He'd make her suffer somehow though, maybe tell her his knee slapping anecdotes from his golf course misadventures for four days straight. It seemed all Amara truly feared was boredom. I envied that in her.

I rose my head a little above water.

"Then Cincinnati hits a home run and comes a cunt hair away from winning," the drunk white-haired man in the member's only jacket said to the heavy set woman wearing a visor on her head and a fanny pack around her waist. They talked with mid-western, particularly Ohio accents yet dressed like tourists and stayed at the Ramada Inn. This confused me at first then Amara whispered, her lips teasing my ear lobe as she spoke, "They're having an affair." The old man's arms were locked with hers as they walked past the pool, out the gate, and into the parking lot without so much as glimpsing in our direction.

"Thank God." I climbed down to the patio from the hot tub and covered myself with the hotel towel, insufficient in length and width as usual.

"I rented another room," she told me.

"Come again?" I blinked rapidly, baffled half to death.

"When I arrived," Amara sat on the edge of the Jacuzzi, "before I went upstairs to meet Luther, I rented my own room, under an assumed name of course." She dangled her long bronze legs over the side of the hot tub. "Why don't you come up for a drink?"

"I'll pass." I started to walk off.

"I'm not trying to get you drunk. I brought a 2-liter of Diet Coke just for you."

The statement melted me. How was I to decline?

"You slept with her, didn't you?" Paul's voice resounded through the motel room darkness as I tried to enter quietly. Much to my chagrin Paul and I were roommates for this little break in Luther's wild ride. Knowing what a mess he'd been after Cincinnati, I'd rather have shared quarters with Mad Dog.

The light between the beds flashed on. Paul sat up in his skivvies, his sheets pulled back, that same "you've screwed up again" expression reddening his boney face. I didn't feel like hearing it.

"Screwed who?" I lied at first. "I was in the hot tub."

"And so was she. Our window looks directly down onto the pool."

I sighed, dropping my towel on the floor. My underwear had dried by now. "And?"

"And I saw everything. The embrace. The kiss." When Paul mentioned the kiss, he made a ridiculous pantomime, closing his eyes, kissing the air and fondling an invisible set of tits. "Then you two disappeared. It's been over an hour and you just now showed up. What's so goddamn funny?"

"I'm sorry." I tried to catch my breath. "I'm still laughing at that stupid little impression you did a minute ago. Was that supposed to NOT make me laugh?"

"Jon. There are several murders in which we've been involved."

"Will you keep your damn voice down? Luther and Amara are right next door."

"Luther's passed out. What do you think? The mere whiff of her angelic loins woke him up with an unearthly desire for sloppy seconds."

The dialogue ended. Paul's anger fled. He knew he'd gone too far because, as he could always tell, I really liked her.

"I'm sorry." He shook his head. "I'm just keyed up."

"It's okay. I mean, I barely know her so to throw down in fisticuffs with my best friend over one offensive remark would be kind of sophomoric don't you think."

"Sophomoric?" Paul did the laughing now. "Yeah, that would be a bit sophomoric. Kind of like dealing Addies to an unpredictable rich kid tweeker. Kind of like thinking you're the heroin kingpin of Louisville before you'd even made one deal, an assumption which, might I add, resulted in the deaths of several people."

"Wait a damn minute. We're going to go into the archives again? Did you not hear a word Milligan and Luther said to you?"

"I heard it. Yes. I didn't exactly buy it. The 'break a few eggs' speech?"

Paul tramped across the room in his boxers. We both stood face to face in front of the dresser and television, only inches between us. "I definitely heard what he said loud and clear. We're stuck. If we try to ever get out of this life, he and Milligan will bury us."

"We'll worry about that when the time comes." I fell onto my bed and closed my eyes.

"And then what do we do?" Paul asked, standing beside my bed.

"Don't you remember what Mad Dog told us," I said. "A good defense is a lethal offense. If it comes to it, we act first."

25

WE SPENT THE end of the week eating well at the Columbia Steakhouse across from the motel and the country diner attached to the Ramada. Whenever Luther would drink himself legless, I'd sneak over to Amara's secret room. This always caused Paul sweat-filled, short-breathed panic attacks. But in my usual selfish fashion, I put my supposed needs over his own perhaps more realistic ones.

On Saturday we drove to Chicago. Luther road with Amara in his Range Rover he'd had her drive up while us hired hands took the El Dorado.

Unlike Roach, Sergei spared no expense. Upon entering Maido, the Japanese / American fusion place in Wicker Park where he'd requested we arrive by four p.m., Mad Dog told us to prepare to be truly wined and dined. Outside kids on slate boards flew by. Young men wearing pants as tight as their girlfriends walked past.

Amara had left us to go shopping. Luther handed her a roll of hundreds and pinched her left ass cheek, marking his territory in front of his men and any passers by like the prehistoric mammal I'd learned him to be. I'd liked Luther a lot more when we were just drinking buddies who tooted lines of high-grade cocaine together, wrestled in dive bar parking lots, and kicked in SUV windows on dares. Now that, with no hope of recourse, karma forced me to watch him treat a woman I'd fallen for like a new Caddy he wanted to show off, I couldn't help but wish him ill, and envision myself taking everything. His business, his woman, and his house in the suburbs painted cowardly yellow.

The inside of Maido, ultra-modern, looked like the control room of the Death Star, all steel and plastic, the tables thin, their legs wiry. A short, beer gutted bald man arose from a long table in the back, snapping his fingers and waving like a tourist. He wore an immaculate double-breasted suit as did the two substantially taller men who'd risen with him, their hands crossed over their jackets like secret service agents protecting the president. He must have recognized Luther's hat.

We sat and ordered drinks. Sergei insisted on a round of Vodka shots for the entire table. I whispered that there would be none for me to the trendy waiter then apologized to Sergei.

"What's wrong with this one?" Sergei pointed at me without the slightest fear of offense. "He afraid of lil' drop of Russian vodka. He little girl? What?" He slapped my forearm. "He not know whether that's small cock between legs or large clit'ris?" Sergei certainly amused himself, turning and slapping both his men hard between their shoulders. Either of these men, both standing over six feet tall, all pure corded muscle, in any other circumstance, would hand the fat boy's head to him on a platter for laying a hand on them. But Sergei was the brains and paid their expenses so they took it.

I cataloged the look the bodyguard to Sergei's left displayed the moment the boss man turned his attention back to his guests. The Russian thug's nostrils flared and his eyelids twitched, stretching the crescent moon scar that ran from the corner of his mouth to his ear lobe.

"This man..." Luther jerked a thumb at me. "Is the one who is going to iron out most of the details of this deal we're making here."

"Oh." Sergei laughed heartily again. "Is that so? Vagina man have big brains to make up for his lack of cock."

I looked at Paul who shook his head. Don't lose your cool. Not here. Not now. I nodded in acquiescence.

"When he drinks," Mad Dog explained, "he can't think tactically." Mad Dog twirled his finger next to his temple, the universal sign for crazy. "He loses his logic."

"Ahhh," Sergei said. "Seems many like that in this country. You people should learn to handle your shit better, man."

I forced a smile. I wanted to pull off my belt, strangle Sergei to death, then shoot up as much of his China White as you please.

Instead I informed him of the horses idea.

"You own land in Peoria, Illinois, correct?" I asked him. "Several acres?"

Sergei looked at me as if I asked if his daughter was for sale and how much. Mad Dog immediately moved his right hand closer to his left hip where he concealed a .38 Smith and Wesson in a quick-draw rig.

"How do you know of my country holdings?" Sergei drank his shot. Automatically upon noticing his drained glass, his bodyguard on his right snapped his fingers at our passing server and pointed at the glass.

"I'm a cop," Mad Dog whispered, his hand still positioned to pull on the Russians, kill all three in this crowded high-end bistro. That would be a hard one to cover up or avoid backlash later considering the full restaurant of witnesses and the yuppie neighborhood. One wrong move here today could easily wind us up dead or in prison, easier than the shootouts on the banks of the Ohio and in the Cinci ghetto to which, as far as I knew and as far as Mad Dog had heard in local cop gossip, no one had linked to any of Luther's crew.

It was sad, but I had begun to accept violence, found myself drawn to blood as I did the power, the wheeling and dealing. For a sick moment, I almost hoped Mad Dog killed all the Russians. I knew Luther's whole enterprise would someday head south, at least for all involved but the boss man. The middle management always got screwed.

"Dirty cop." Sergei laughed, disdainfully glaring at the nervous waiter refilling the shot glasses, offering me another soda which I declined. "The only useful police I know. Cheers, Detective Milligan."

Sergei raised his glass and drank before allowing anyone else to toast.

"I think I have a cheap idea of how to expand your enterprise south without fear of your transporters taking much heat from the Highway Patrol," I said. "But it'll take some structuring and some foresight."

This was the beginning of Luther's most lucrative period as a drug lord. By the end of the night we had a deal. Sergei would enter the horse racing business, mainly on a sales level, driving to Kentucky for thoroughbreds and selling them to trainers and more experienced owners from Southern Chicago all the way to the contacts he'd cultivated in Memphis and Nashville. The entire South would be run by Luther who'd act as the overseer of Sergei's legitimate business, and the one solely responsible for making sure the dope hid in the wheel wells of the horse trailers stayed purer than anything north of Memphis, the hungriest markets since the government had cracked down on pills, making it virtually impossible for an addict to stay high on Oxies, Percocets, or Tabs.

Sergei began to look at me a little different now, a certain respect in the lifeless dark of his expression, but a weary respect, as if he knew I'd stay a step ahead of the rest and that I was prepared to do what I needed to be the one who didn't suffer if we took heat.

If he'd ever said any of this out loud to me, at the time, considering the wisdom of mourning I've known since, I'd have told him that no matter what, no one escapes suffering in a life like the one we'd all chosen.

"Maybe he does have dick." Sergei shoveled a heap of stir fry into his mouth which he'd already half filled with a chunk of what the menu called an "American Egg Roll," which I couldn't help but think was just some chef's renaming of cheese sticks.

Luther said, "Who's gonna pull over a horse trailer? Interfering with the horse trade in the bluegrass is basically sacrilegious. On top of that, the only people we gonna actually meet face to face will be legitimate businessmen. The other deliveries will be picked up in the middle of the night while the trailers are parked, cash taped in place of the product then returned via the same trailer to Louisville, then to you here in Chi town minus our cut."

"Speaking of cuts." Sergei placed his fork on his empty plate. "Since I provide the basis for this entire operation, I feel half would be more than fair."

Mad Dog stood to leave. This part of the business would be left to those in charge. And me. I was asked to remain while the rest stood outside to smoke.

I got Sergei down to forty percent.

"You're like a son to me, kid," Luther lied as we walked out to meet our crew out front, leaving Sergei with the bill despite Luther's feigned protests. "My fucking golden boy."

26

THE FIRST TRIPS went smoothly. We'd park the trailers at some fleabag hotel lot a few miles from where we were to meet our legitimate horse owners and trainers or even those just hopeful to make a name for themselves in the industry. The transportation, at first, was left to me, Jimmy, and Paul. We all rode armed, but mercy had somehow graced us as each transaction went better than any one of us could have hoped.

Sometimes I easily forgot Mad Dog Mulligan was a police sergeant, head of a FLEX Unit responsible for more drug arrests than any other narcotics division in the city. Unless we were dealing with someone new, he never road along. To be honest, I missed the bastard. Mad Dog was a loyal soldier with instincts one only believed possible in a Bruce Lee film.

But he had a day job, one crucial to his nefarious night-time deviations from the code he'd sworn and broken so many years ago when he stopped believing in the law.

"My legacy ain't gonna be that of a man who protects the haves from the have nots," he'd told me on the car ride back to Louisville from our first meet with the Russians. I pointed out the Hemingway reference to which he explained, "Hemingway will always be dear to me. The few times in my life I've considered eating my gun I remembered that Papa waited at least until his sixties to punch his own ticket. Forced myself to do the same thing."

"And how old are you now?" Paul had joked, checking his watch as if counting the seconds until the detective's 60th birthday so we could finally be rid of him.

Irina hadn't called in weeks, not since my grandiose re-entrance into her life and, quickly thereafter, our final kiss off, my back turned as I left her standing on her steps holding flowers and the payment of my debt that she'd held over my head for a year.

I knew it was just a matter of time.

I'd slept half that day, tired from a run to Knoxville with Paul, loading and unloading heroin and horses, watching Paul drink himself stupid in some small town bar outside of the city, preventing him from escalating two conflicts with a pair of bikers and then a trucker, both parties fully capable of slaughtering us.

The phone had rang several times that morning and I'd let it go to voicemail. Amara was at the store watching over things and I had desperately needed the privacy and rest. Finally, around three, I answered the umpteenth phone call, thinking Luther needed me, that something had gone wrong and more heinous acts against humanity needed committing.

I answered without glancing the caller ID.

"Don't hang up" were her first words.

"Irina?" I wasn't surprised to hear from her, but I'd never heard her sound so drained and desolate.

"I just wanted to talk. Do you have a minute?"

I prayed she wasn't pregnant and started counting, in my mind, how long it had been since we'd last slept together.

"Sure." I sat on the edge of the couch where I'd passed out from seemingly fatal exhaustion the night before. "Just let me rub my eyes a second. I've had a long week and was just resting."

"I miss you." She was crying now. "And I'm worried. Where did you get that money? I haven't seen you with that much cash since you opened the store."

"Things are picking up," I lied.

She knew. She said so. "I always know when you're lying. When are you going to learn that? Either refuse to tell me or tell the truth."

"Don't worry about me. I'm fine. Believe it or not, I've been sober over two months."

"That part I buy. You looked great when you stopped by."

I found that old stirring feeling entwining my heart, stomach, and loins.

But all was lost between us. She'd never come back knowing the life I'd entered. And furthermore, she'd never be safe if for some reason she stuck around, fully cognizant of what I'd become.

"Are you in trouble, Jon?" she asked. "It's never too late to turn things around."

I couldn't help it. I laughed out loud, right into the receiver. Never too late. If she only knew.

"I gotta get ready for work." I began slipping on my dirty jeans that I'd left crumpled at the foot of the couch.

"I love you." She began crying again.

I muttered goodbye and hung up on her.

Jimmy had gotten real bad, real quick. Today he could barely walk. He'd be leading a horse onto the trailer and let go of the reign, stumbling against the white gates that separated and surrounded the animals, laughing at himself while the horse for which he'd been responsible ran free, Paul and I chasing after. Mad Dog, despite his affection for the recently freed felon, had expressed concern over my old friend's renewed and severely progressive habit.

Occasionally, I'd allow Luther to conduct transactions at the bookstore. Only his most trusted business associates were allowed to make deals in this manner, usually country boys done good who dressed well and sold out in the county, characters who wouldn't look completely out of place in a bookstore. They'd come in inquiring about a specific set of dictionaries. Amara or I would have already cut deep rectangles into the pages in which to hide the dope. On the outside, they resembled any other books. Whoever was working that day, me, my two best friends, or my little dark-haired coffin nail, would help the buyer load their purchase, amicable goodbyes were shared, and we wouldn't see them until the next month when perhaps they felt in the mood for leatherbound copies of Dickens' entire omnibus.

The last time Detective Mad Dog Milligan joined me to oversee the operation, he'd asked of Jimmy's whereabouts. Despite my recent sobriety, I hated ratting out a fellow junkie. Instead I hung my head and asked

Mad Dog if he ever got tired of looking for answers to questions that he already knew.

"The guy's been useful to us." Mad Dog kicked at a bale of hay outside of one of the barns at Luther's new, massive horse farm just outside of town. We'd been sitting around, smoking cigarettes and telling lies after a long and rushed run to Nashville and back, speeding to make it to Louisville in time to buy more horses for Sergei to sell.

"No one can make him stop." To this day, I wish I'd never expressed one hint of concern that Jimmy might soon become a liability. I knew Mad Dog, no matter how cool he seemed as of late, reported everything he heard back to Luther.

"You don't think I know the nature of addiction." Mad Dog slowly traipsed through the knee high witch grass where he'd parked a new Lincoln he'd bought since our first few deals. "My daddy was a fucking drunkard." This was the most intimate thing Mad Dog ever said to me, and the moment had passed before I realized.

Paul just sat there staring at the hoof beat mud. "Liabilities and assets. That's how these men look at things."

"That's how all business works." I stomped my cigarette into the mud.

"Not all business is life or death."

27

WHILE LUTHER ASSEMBLED an army of drivers and farm workers, Jimmy, Paul, and I all agreed to still help with transportation a couple of more weeks, making sure the new guys knew what they were doing. It seemed my job got harder, breaking in the new blood, because rather than just do the job myself or with Paul or Jimmy, I had to explain everything, sometimes to a complete dolt from the hills that Luther had hired, probably kin. Sometimes I'd stay away from the store for weeks at a time, executing runs from Chicago to Louisville and Lexington, all the way down to Memphis. During this transition period, Luther asked me to let Amara help run the bookstore and the moment I agreed I knew that I'd just willingly invited a tidal flood of heart attack level stress into my life.

As we walked along the river back toward Luther's car where I'd continued playing designated driver and escort for him to some other dive, I watched the rushing waters of the Ohio and could envision the water whisking me along the banks, Amara sitting on the Kennedy bridge gesticulating, ordering the waves' movement as an evil conductor might a maddened orchestra.

If, under circumstances of such heightened security, I couldn't keep my hands off the lover of Louisville's most ruthless gangster, what was I to do when the cuckold had just offered me an opportunity to spend twice as much time with her, most of it unsupervised.

"She loves the place, man," Luther told me at the Air Devil's Inn as I sipped my club soda and pretended to listen to him talk about himself. When he said the name of his cousin / lover who I had been bedding for close to a month, my ears perked. "She was showing me these pictures she has in an old photo collection. Some Jewish weirdo that knew Hemingway and had places for all those Paris pansies to hang out."

"Gertrude Stein," I said. "Owned a lot of parlors in Paris and London."

"Parlor." Luther snapped his fingers. "That's what Amara called it. Damn, that girl's too smart for her own damn good. I'm not doing wonders for the clichés about Kentucky, I know, shacking up with my cousin. But, for the love of sweet baby Jesus, Jon. Have you ever met anyone like her?"

I paused in reverence, as if we were speaking of the Mother Mary or Joan of Arc, minus the piety aspect.

"No." I couldn't think of anything else to say.

"She needs something to do all day besides drink and wait for me to come home and swim with her and tell dirty jokes and try to bed her."

I clenched my fist. But then I considered how little emphasis he put on their sex life. Was she really not sleeping with him as she'd promised me? Had she really lost any ability to let him touch her since she and I had begun our affair? The problem was, I couldn't ask him. Anything that remotely placed Luther's manhood in question could result in multiple homicide.

Luckily the man had gotten drunk enough to spill his guts.

"She's young." Luther's tone turned grave. "Had a rough coming up. Whole family of felons, child diddlers, and meth heads. Grew up over in Cumberland where most of my people come from. If you ask me, the girl's come a long way."

I knew all about Amara. How she'd escaped Cumberland, gotten a full ride at the University of Louisville studying English.

"Girl got her a college degree." Luther ordered another high-ball.

"Only one in the Longmire clan ever to pull that off. She knows her books and she's proven she can make sales. I know that ain't your main source of income no more, but if your store looks like it's doing well, it'll make a little more sense you living a little better. No one will ask where the money came from. Her looks don't hurt nothing either. Most men would buy a book there every day just to look at those legs."

I agreed to hire her as my new manager. Luther had sold me. She was good to have around anyway. We'd get to spend more time in the overstock closet.

28

MAD DOG WARNED us, "This is one despicable human being you three are meeting today. If you could call him that." It was Derby time in Louisville and half the police in town, even detectives and sergeants of specialized units, were dressed in Kevlar vests over their full police blues, ready for all out war. Around the city's worst neighborhoods, rioting and automatic weapon fire became common, ghetto celebration, same with the Fourth of July. Mad Dog crossed his arms, leaning on the hood of his marked unit, turning his head west toward where most of the sinister Derby partying would occur. He'd driven us out to Luther's farm, met us on the edge of the property where we'd set up a generator outside a small shed along with a table and a cooler of beer. The meeting would be over long before dark, and the light from the small windows would suffice for our purposes.

Instead of moving the dope with the horse trailers, we'd simply buried it a few yards from the shed. Today, we were to explain to this maniac Tyrone Cotton, who'd taken Rig's place as King of the Wild West End, the price changes and other modifications with which he'd have to come to terms unless he wanted us to supply some other mope with the best heroin in town.

"If this fellow's so awful, then why are we the ones assigned to deal with him?" Paul checked the load on his newest piece, a bright silver .22 Mad Dog had found on some suspect and pocketed the night before. "I think maybe you'd be better suited to handle a murderous, meth head pimp, considering you already know the fellow."

"Paul, I have to work," Mad Dog said.

"Oh, that job where you arrest the clients we depend on for this job right here." Paul forced a chortle. "Sometimes I forget that you're so much more than just a bag man." Paul always reacted to fear and stress either via irksome complaint or biting humor.

Mad Dog opened the door to his cruiser and leaned against the top of the window sill. "Also, guys, you made this bed and you're going to have to lie in it. I used to run protection for Rig and make sure that Louisville's west end didn't have a complete monster running the dope trade. If certain parties hadn't decided to take a crash course in criminal behavior, Rig might still be around and we could still be dealing with him. As of now, Tyrone runs the wild west and until we find someone more suitable to replace him, he's a necessary evil."

"Jimmy's not coming?" I knew what an exercise in futility arguing with the detective always turned out. I tried to keep today's talks with him terse.

Mad Dog entered the car, rolled down the driver's side window. "We sometimes forget, Jimmy saved Luther's life in Cinci. Jimmy's shitting in high cotton. Luther's got them a table at millionaire's row."

Shit, I thought. If Luther saw what horrible shape Jimmy was in these days, he might shed his gratitude over what the junkie had done for him in Cincinnati. Before a limo escorted them to Churchill Downs, Longmire and Jimmy had dropped off all of Luther's paperbacks at the store for Amara to stock and inventory. When she called my cell before my sit-down with Tyrone she told me he'd also surprised her with two tickets to Paris. I felt nauseated. I now made enough money to take the girl to Europe every other month but I couldn't because a chuck and jive cowboy had some sort of hold on her via blood and money. I diverted my thoughts elsewhere, back to this concern over, according to my favorite dirty cop, the mental soundness of the man who'd arrive here any minute to retrieve his re-up.

I reconsidered what we knew about Cotton, the verbal dossier Mad Dog had recited: "The brother's got at least six bodies on him that no one in homicide can pin. The Scourge of Clarksdale is the nickname beat cops had given the young player sometime in the mid-90s." Mad Dog had explained that, growing up in the now torn down Clarksdale projects had been the best education a budding psychopath could hope for. "Mother addicted to smack. Father a PCP peddler. You'd almost feel bad for the guy if you never saw the photographs of his handiwork." Mad Dog lamented those who'd fallen out with the Scourge as Cotton had been nicknamed growing up on the mean riverside streets just north of downtown. "He likes baseball bats. Carries a piece, but if he has his druthers, he always opts to use his bare hands or a Louisville Slugger."

"There he is." Paul nodded toward the Dodge Stratus pulling off the state route, onto the mile-long gravel road that led to the shed. The southern periphery of Luther's farm ended at the corrugated fence that lined the gravel. We were told to not mention the farm. The only living things anywhere near were the cows that grazed in the surrounding fields. The warehouses of the farm couldn't be seen from here and for good reason.

"Who wants a mass murderer to know where to find you?" Mad Dog had asked.

The red Stratus parked a few feet short of the shed. The sight of the driver stopped us in our tracks as we descended the sagging plank steps from the shed to meet Cotton's entourage in the neglected front yard.

The kid was a spitting image of young Ty who Paul and I had shot to death, Ty if he'd gotten to go to the Derby, to dress up in a light brown suit, his tie perfectly fitted by his mother or aunt or whichever broken down project woman had raised this kid. The tallest of Cotton's crew stood beside the teenager. This was the only one who'd neglected to dress to the nines. He wore Hilfiger from ankle to neck, jean shorts and a glittery T-shirt. When the back door opened, I immediately recognized LMPD's most wanted from the burn marks that discolored the right side of his face, an injury sustained when his mother left her cigarette ablaze and passed out from a two week crack binge, burning down not just their unit, but every section 8 apartment on the block. Cotton removed his black hat that matched his searsucker suit and said, "The book man, I presume."

Paul's eyes stayed locked on the teenage driver, the dead Cincinnati boy's doppelganger.

The meeting went better than expected. I dug up Cotton's dope. He unfastened the consoles on both front doors of his Stratus and paid us. We agreed from then on to deliver, for him alone, to The Green Room, the strip club on South Seventh Street where Cotton ran his whores. "I ain't gonna fit in too well trying to play off like I'm a horse or faggot book enthusiast." Cotton explained. "However, The Green Room being so close to the track, we meet, act like I'm helping y'all buy some hay or supplies or horse dick condoms or whatever and when we head our separate ways, you boys got cash money and I got my Ron."

The kid's name was Myron. The muscle in the Hilfiger went by Bub. We all smiled and shook hands. When's Paul's palm touched Myron's, he bit his lip and swallowed hard.

"Think you gonna make any money today?" The boy Myron asked. "They got one of them off betting tracks just down..."

The kid ruined his suit falling in the mud. I hadn't realized Tyrone had struck him until Paul reached to the small of his back for his new automatic. Bub's hand disappeared beneath his coat. Cotton's muscle had noticed Paul's attempt to draw. I grabbed Paul's forearm and forced it away from his back. Bub loosened up, removing his hand, gun free, from his coat.

"You think these two give a motherfuck about anything you gotsa to say, boy?" Cotton stood over the kid who remained lying in the mud, anticipating a kick or two which Cotton then delivered. "I told yo' no good sister I'd take you on one condition. Now repeat to me what she made you promise."

"That I wouldn't do n-nuthin' uh-unless," Myron made eye contact with his boss and stuttered, "you said to do something fuh-first."

"Now shut up and get back in the vehicle." Cotton ambled through the weeds over to the passenger side then shouted back at his nephew, "You done ruined your suit. Now I'm gonna have to drive myself over to Loretta's party. Her daughter fancied you, boy, but I guess since you done fucked up and spoke out of turn I'm gonna have to knock the dust off both them pussies."

Paul was shaking.

I couldn't tell Luther, but we had a big problem on our hands now.

29

AMARA'S SOFT TOUCH and hard love eased much of the fatigue that resulted from suffering fools for the majority of my week. We'd been considering an elaborate lie that would allow us to get out of town together, but until the day I met Tyrone Cotton face-to-face and realized the ticking time bomb Paul had become since we'd killed the kid in Ohio, I hadn't taken seriously the thought of vacation.

"I already told him my aunt Serena has entered the nuthouse again and I have to get down to Cumberland to help with damage control." Amara appeared overjoyed that she'd set-up an alibi and could leave town safely. "Now you need to come up with something."

Unfortunately, my only thought involved switching with Paul on Friday and allowing him to go with Hagan out to Mount Washington to deliver a nag to Tyrone Cotton's cousin and make the week's trade. Despite what the psychopath had said, as crazies were known to do, he'd changed his mind and wanted the same deal everyone else got, a horse buying front for our exchanges.

From there, hauling the dope back to the city was Tyrone's problem. I hesitated allowing Paul to take my place considering last week's conversation at Air Devil's Inn:

Paul: Doesn't it ever keep you up nights?

Me: What? The men we've killed? The kid in Cincinnati? Or sleeping with Luther's paramour?

Paul: How do you sleep at all?

Me: Nyquil.

Paul: This weekend, I had Adam. Took him over to the skateboard park. Every time I looked in his eyes, you know what I saw?

Me: The kid we shot.

Paul: No. That kid Myron that works for Luther's new head man in the wild west. That kid who is going to wind up just like Roach's boy if someone doesn't get him out of the life.

Me: Don't go borrowing trouble. It's none of our business.

Paul snorted, finished his drink, gave me the shit eye and left the tab for me to pay.

Yet despite this horrible omen, the knowledge that Paul might do something stupid if Myron took another beating in front of him, did not stop me from whisking Amara away to Austin where we ate crawfish, made love in pools, hot tubs and lakes, and cried together when we discovered we had to come home after reading in the Courier Journal about the discovery of Tyrone Cotton's corpse along with his cousin Bub's and that of an unidentified white male in the trunk of Cotton's own Dodge Stratus which police found abandoned on the top floor of the Louisville airport's parking garage.

I knew I'd hear from Paul before Amara and I made it halfway to Texarkana in our rented SUV.

What I didn't expect was to find Sergei and Luther browsing the bookshelves of my store, discussing murder.

30

I THANKED GOD the bookstore had huge windows. There would've been two murders to discuss had I walked in holding hands with Luther's mistress. While Amara sped east in our rented Cherokee, I entered my business and did a forced double-take when I found Luther and Sergei both sitting cross-legged in the arm chairs of the reading area.

Jimmy had covered for me all week and, as far as I knew, Luther had no idea I'd been out of town.

Sergei, Luther, and I shared polite hellos and how-ya-doings, then Luther invited me to sit down in my own place, the kind of gesture only a man with a severely twisted ego could express so lackadaisically. I wheeled the front desk swivel around and pushed it a few yards to form a triangle with the two gangsters lounging in my armchairs.

Last minute, Sergei had decided to send one of his men down from Chicago to make the run with Paul and Jimmy south, just to supervise the operation to which the Russians were now partner.

Ivan, Sergei's cousin, drove with Paul and Jimmy— they'd closed the store a little earlier to make the run —hauling a trailer full of thoroughbreds destined for Mount Washington along with one nag for Mr. Cotton. The convoy first stopped in Bardstown, about forty miles east of the bookstore, to make Cotton's drop.

Besides our men, Cotton and Myron were present, waiting at an abandoned truck stop just off Route 31. This time, besides the lack of church attire, there was something different about Myron. The kid walked with a limp and when Paul shook his hand, two of the teenager's fingers were missing.

I suppose Paul thought of his son again.

After the money and dope had been exchanged, when Paul leaned forward to shake hands with Cotton, he drew the .22 Mad Dog had given him Derby weekend and shot the Scourge of Clarksdale four times. Because killing Myron would only defeat Paul's purpose, he waited for the late Cotton's young driver to try and draw and pistol whipped the kid, kicking the gun into the nearby shrubbery.

"That's the thanks I get for killing your abusive surrogate father?" Paul had asked, according to what Jimmy had told Luther and Mad Dog when they arrived in Bardstown to help Jimmy drive the trailers back to home base, just the two of them, Paul and Myron long ago disappeared.

They'd peeled out in Cotton's Dodge.

"Don't kill me." Cotton's teenage punching bag had covered his face.

Jimmy drew his piece. He hadn't known what to do as his loyalty leaned closer to me and he knew the lengths I'd go to avenge the killing of a brother which is how I'd referred to Paul for years now.

"Please." While pleading, Myron's voice stayed calm, trying to reason with the killer rather than beg. "I'll disappear. I ain't gonna tell no one what you done, man."

Jimmy fired once in the air, part of the story he didn't tell Luther, to warn Paul of the imminent shotgun blast. Paul already knew Ivan had his hands on the gun. Paul spun, knelt, took a few moments to aim, and fired once.

Faceless, the Russian slumped against one of ancient, empty gas pumps.

Paul's tenure as lieutenant for Luther Longmire officially ended when he killed Ivan.

So far, everything Luther had said jived with Paul's fevered telling of the events. Before I'd arrived at the store, while Amara and I were somewhere in the woods of Arkansas, Paul had called from a blocked number. I didn't ask him where he was hiding and he didn't offer. That way, in case Mad Dog did all the questioning, I didn't have to tell a lie the detective would sniff out before I'd even spoken a few syllables.

Luther ashed his cigar on my rug. I'd begun to equate these expensive carpets with cigarette lighters, interchangeable and disposable. "Then your boy loaded the bodies in the trunk, threw the nigger kid in Cotton's charger and high-tailed it back to the interstate."

"Where is this Paul?" Sergei hadn't blinked since I'd arrived. He'd stared through me for so long now, I wondered if he'd named my entrails.

"Sergei." Luther lightly patted the back of the chair where our supplier sat on the edge, his hands clasped on his knees, tapping his foot, ready to act on any information I could give him in regards to my best friend. "We agreed, at least for a little bit, I'd do the talking."

Luther winked at me, unbuttoned his blazer to show off the hand canon shoved down into his waistband. "Me and Johnny here go back." Then he directed his attention my way again. "Don't panic. Jon my boy, we ain't out no money or dope, so no one believes this was a robbery."

"We actually made some money." I always spoke quietly when fighting to curb my sardonic wit. "We got Cotton's money and kept our..." Rarely did lowering the volume of my voice assist me in sounding less like a smug smartass. "And we didn't have to let go of those horses." I never spoke of drugs explicitly inside the store, over the phone, or even anywhere public that hadn't been cased. Better to be to careful than butt raped by a gangbanger or a member of the Aryan Brotherhood disgruntled that you wouldn't join the white power prison ranks. "We've got ourselves free money and horses we can resell." Since I'd first released into the ether my idea of using the horse racing as a front for Luther's real money-making enterprise, we always referred to heroin as horse, or even specific breeds: "These thoroughbred's better not have too many miles on them" Luther's contact in Memphis would ask assurance over the purity of our heroin.

"Heh heh heh." Sergei removed a tin flask from the inner pocket of his suit coat. "Funny. Making funnies at time like this." Sergei swigged from the flask. "Luther, you didn't tell me your main lieutenant was a woman or that she had a sense of humor. I love funny women. Bitches usually have no funny in them." Sergei toasted me. "This one though should do stand-up."

"A man after my own heart," I said to Sergei. "Us

185

women, all we want is to be heard. And it's good to know you're listening, Sergei. I'm also comforted to believe that you can see what we've gained here."

I'd somehow managed, over the previous months, to suffocate my fear. Watching almost ten men die, killing some of them myself, might have made me a bit more immune to buckling under the pressure of the constant threat of death. The man I'd been a year ago would be begging Sergei for my life right now, perhaps even offering up my best friend. The man I'd been definitely wouldn't have sassed the maniac from Moscow. I honestly meant no offense to either Luther or Sergei. But I did feel it prudent to point out what benefits Paul's poorly considered actions might have brought. Humor perhaps had not been the best medium through which to express my message.

"Because none of the product or cash came up missing is why you still possess all your limbs." Luther had dropped his salesman persona. He'd reverted back to pure killer, the same man who'd shoved a drunk and surly stripclubber's customer's nose bone into his brain when Luther was just a lowly bouncer with delusions of grandeur.

"I ain't got a dog in this race," Luther continued. "Not personally, at least. As you said, Jon, we ain't lost no money or horses. However, we now have a power vacuum in the West End, our strongest local market. And we got no one to fill it, no one in our pocket at least. That's what Mad Dog's working on right now, going through rap sheets and other files down at the narcotics headquarters over on Barrett, finding someone who might have the brains and, pardon the pun, track record to handle our weight."

"I may have someone for you," I said.

Luther yielded one of those expressions that usually belongs to the last face a dying man ever sees. "Did either of us ask you any kind of question?

"No." I hung my head and closed my eyes out of respect for the man who'd helped save my bookstore, heightened my lifestyle exponentially, and prevented my death in that Cincinnati ambush last month. "I just..."

"You just need to wait until I tell you I'm ready to hear you talk," Luther said.

I nodded affirmatively.

"Ivan was my brother's son." Sergei entwined his fingers tightly as if praying for his kin's loss. "My nephew. I held him seconds after he's born. No amount of money can repay this loss. You must find your friend. You must kill him."

Sergei drove off in his black BMW 5-Series, headed toward Baxter Avenue from where he could reach Broadway and the interstate that would take him back home to Chicago. I smoked a cigarette on the front steps of my bookstore while Luther clarified Sergei's words spoken with such lethal finality.

"You don't have to do it yourself," Luther reassured me. "But Paul screwed the pooch in this one, son. I'm sorry he had a soft spot for little, neglected ghetto teenagers. I know Paul has his own teenage son and that's why I worked so hard to get the Russians to let us handle this. You know how Sergei would proceed right now if I hadn't promised him your assistance?"

I shuddered at the thought but asked, "How?"

"He'd go grab up Paul's son and mail the mother a finger every other weekday until Paul surfaced."

I stumbled upward, finally finding my own two feet, telling Luther, "Anything happens to that kid, I'll kill all that ruskie fuck's other nephews, just for starters."

"Nothing's gonna happen to Paul's kid." Luther laughed. "But Paul's gotta pay."

"With his life?" My voice cracked. "You go around talking loyalty and here you stand asking me to sign my best friend's death warrant like you were bumming a cigarette."

The word loyalty brought to mind how I'd done Longmire, catting around with his woman while he helped make me a fortune.

"Given our options..." Luther stared fixedly in the direction in which Sergei had driven off. "Mutilating Paul's son, a war with the Russians, our Chicago connections drying up... letting go of Paul is, sadly, the best. He made his bed. And if I were you, Jon, and I found him, I'd kill him rather than turn him into Sergei. I told Jimmy and Milligan the same thing."

"Why?"

"Because a bullet to the brain is mercy compared to what Sergei has in mind for your friend."

31

PAUL AND MYRON, both now fugitives from the Dixie mafia in Louisville and the Russians in Chicago, had formed a strained partnership, a dynamic that reminded me how a TV show would turn out if some brilliant Hollywood television writer fused *The Odd Couple* with *The Wire*.

"Fucking kid still watches cartoons." Paul sat in a lawn chair by the swimming pool of the Residential Inn, a pay-by-the-week hotel just across the Ohio River in Jeffersonville, part of a row of strip malls, chain restaurants, and lodgings of a similar class. "He's almost old enough to die in a war and he watches cartoons."

"What I don't understand," I said, "is how he got over you shooting his boss to death and rendering him a Russian mafia target?"

"He had a long car ride from Bardstown to consider how Cotton had treated him." From the airport where they'd left the bodies, Paul had rented a Ford Focus to get them across the river. Paul had reverted back to his panicked state of shaking his leg and lighting one cigarette after the other. The tops of the dogwood trees at the pool's edge blocked the view of the river and the three bridges that anytime could lead Paul to the death that Luther and Sergei wished upon him or vice versa. "And I'll admit, I used my well honed skills of manipulation to help put things in a better perspective for him."

"What exactly does said perspective entail?"

"We help make Myron the new king of wild west Louisville."

I'd had the same idea.

"Great minds think alike," I said.

I'll admit that Paul's sense of survival and duplicity impressed me quite a bit. This whole time we'd been in the game I'd taken the guy for granted, underestimated him, even had the nerve, on occasion, to consider Paul my sidekick.

Not anymore.

There were a few obstacles in the way of going back to the way things were with Myron stepping into Cotton's place. The first and most inconvenient, of course, Sergei's desire to wash blood with blood.

"If you hadn't killed Ivan, this would be a lot easier to pull off." We'd driven over to the same Waffle House where Mad Dog had treated me to chocolate chip pancakes after we'd killed three people. Myron sat beside me, wolfing down his cheese grits and toast as if he hadn't eaten since Kool and the Gang had first made the Billboard Charts.

"Wasn't really a lot of time to think." Paul finished his third cup of coffee.

The frumpy waitress returned with the pot to refill Paul's cup. I placed my hand to block the flow of coffee and said to her, "He's had enough," then to him, "It's not crack. Lay off for long enough for us to figure how to save our goddamn asses here."

Apparently a religious woman, at the sound of the

Lord's name taken in vein, the waitress drew a hand to her breast and sighed deeply, shocked.

"Nice, Jon," Paul said. "Draw attention to us while there's a contract out on me and the kid."

"I ain't scared." Myron pushed his plate aside and sipped from his soda.

"Have you ever met a Russian, Myron?" Paul asked. Myron nodded "no."

"Okay. Then how do you know you're not scared of them? I mean they're cold, scary people with lifeless shark eyes."

"Now, Paul," I said. "We've ourselves only met a few. And they were from a very specific demographic."

"When we gonna talk about how y'all be making me king?" Myron interrupted me.

All business, what I liked most about the kid so far.

"First, I have to tell a series of well-considered lies to Luther." I reached for my wallet to pay the tab. "Then we head straight to Chicago."

32

I TOLD LUTHER I thought I'd gotten a line on Paul and that, if it was all the same, I'd rather do this job myself. "I brought him into this," I told Luther, us both seated at his same dining room table where we'd solidified our partnership. "He's my responsibility. I'll take care of it."

If Luther sensed any dishonesty on my part, he hid it well. Amara waltzed behind him in a red cotton summer dress, refilling his decanter of whiskey and lightly touching his shoulder. She waited until she was far out of his eyeshot and stopped short of the kitchen doorway to toss her hair across her back, look over her shoulder, and grace me with her hungry eyes.

Luther waited until he knew she'd stepped out of earshot. Then he half-grinned and said, "You never cease to amaze, kid. I can understand. And to boot, I respect your decision. Where do you think that crazy bastard's hiding out?"

"He has people in Upstate New York." This part was true, except all his people there were dead. While I sat here lying my ass off to our boss, Paul was putting Adam on a plane to Cedar Rapids to visit Paul's brother who worked as an English professor at a community college there.

"What about Adam's mother?" I'd asked Paul.

"Anyone who wants to take that bitch out has my

blessing." Paul had turned into a mean son-a-bitch since we'd entered the dope game. And I'd helped.

"So this may take a bit?" Luther asked about my trip to New York.

"I'd say at least a week." If it took us longer than a week to make our play in Chicago, we'd lost anyway. Seven days should have been long enough for the surveillance and planning necessary to execute our scheme.

"What do you need from me?" Luther opened his arms, the loving father offering all he owned to his prodigal son.

And like a junkie who'd steal your wallet then offer to help you search for it, I told him, "Untraceable guns, a good car, and a little cash."

Luther would sponsor my plan to go behind his back tactically.

I'd done worse.

Judging by Sergei's overall decorum during our first introduction, his familiarity with the manager and staff at the restaurant where we'd met him months ago, I figured the best way to find the man would be to stake out the Bistro.

After sitting with Paul and Myron in the Acura Luther had rented us for seven hours straight, two days in a row, I'd already begun to unravel.

We'd arrived early the first two days, found a parking spot just south of the bus stop where we had a clear view of the restaurant's comings and goings. Every so often, one of us would exit the Acura for a coffee or sandwich run, and to make it appear to any passerby that we were doing something other than stalking someone.

Jimmy, who'd at first thought our plan asinine, had finally agreed to join us when I explained Luther's concern with Jimmy's drug use. "If he starts cleaning house with Paul, who knows?" Paul, Myron, and I had swung by Jimmy's mother's house on Deer Lane just a mile east of the bookstore, still near the beating pulse of the hip Highlands. His mom owned a bed and breakfast downtown and was hardly ever home.

"You really think they'd take me out just for my... extra-curricular interests." Jimmy was nodding off on the stairs of the breezeway, nearly falling onto the freshly mowed lawn. But his sense of self-preservation apparently remained strong enough to wake him back up every time he neared comatose. If he hadn't been high, it might not have been so easy to get him to go.

"I think it's likely he'd have your throat slit at a moment's notice," I'd said, which I honestly believed. But Luther would only take out Jimmy if Jimmy cost him money. "You just stay at the hotel, wait for our call, stay high, and back us up if and when we need it."

I'd had him at "stay high."

So while Jimmy shot up, the three of us that weren't currently hooked on intravenous narcotics sat in the Acura and nearly died of slow-creeping malaise.

"Thank God the last few nights have been cool." Paul entered the passenger side and handed out Subway foot-longs.

"This shit sucks." Myron, who'd probably suffered malnutrition his whole life, self-inflicted or at the hands of others, devoured half of his BLT in two bites. With a mouth stiff half full of bacon crumbs and mayo, he continued complaining. "Ain't there no other way to find these commie bitches?"

"Hush up or I'll turn the AC off," I said, as if holding a child's toy hostage to curtail a temper tantrum.

Myron had finished chewing then dropped his jaw to let loose another amalgam of expletives as he had every other time I talked down to him, a production I took great amusement in. He hadn't gotten the first "motherfucker" out when a black Chevrolet Tahoe with tinted windows pulled in front of Maido.

The bodyguard with the scar exited the back seat, holding the door open for Sergei.

I pointed at the disfigured Russian. "That's our man."

The Russians' dinner took two hours and Sergei didn't even have company aside from his hired help. He probably ordered half the menu and polished off two bottles of Vodka, holding his men conversationally hostage, paying them not just for protection, but for company and friendship. He'd probably, as most drunks are apt to do, told the same stories half a dozens times, refusing to acknowledge his employees' misery.

Good, I thought. The more angry Sergei made the man with the scar, the easier the fat Russian drug lord made our job.

Around dark, Sergei's driver walked out Maido's front door and handed the valet the keys to the Tahoe.

"Here we go." I turned the Acura's engine over and sounded a heavy sigh of relief. Waiting for Sergei for the past forty-eight hours had been one of the most boring experiences of all my years sucking air. And like Amara, I hated and dreaded boredom.

"Fuck yeah, bitches." Myron bunched the roof of the Acura waking Paul from his nap.

The Tahoe pulled around and the Russians entered, driving off without offering the valet a tip. The valet quickly flipped them the finger.

"He's lucky Sergei didn't see that." Paul stretched and moved his seat forward. "He doesn't know who he's flipping the bird at."

"Fuck it, man." Myron was bouncing up and down in his seat, excited as an adolescent who'd just found his father's porno stash. "I'm just glad SOMETHING'S finally happening."

"I just hope they don't stop for desert," Paul said.

33

SERGEI DIDN'T DRAG us far. The Tahoe stopped on the western fringe of Wicker Park. Until the Russians pulled into the parking garage of an art deco building of condos across the street from a dog clothing store and a Starbucks, I had no idea the gangster lived in such a swishy neighborhood.

And the guy questioned my masculinity.

I circled the block. "Be on the look for a parking space, boys."

We didn't need one. As I pulled in front of the canopied entrance to the condos, Scarface exited. He headed east, flipping up the collar of his pea coat to shield his sallow skin against the biting river winds that picked up with the Chicago sun's setting.

"Where's he going?" Myron asked.

"I look fucking psychic to you?" I didn't mean to snap at the kid, but cars behind us were honking. I was driving slow, trying to keep Scarface in sight. Thank God he stepped down the stairs of an Irish pub. I told Paul and Myron to get out of the car and find us a table while I parked the SUV.

Myron immediately did as he'd been requested. Paul opened the door, but stopped short of hitting the pavement. "What if he pulls on me? I mean, his boss wants me dead."

I popped the glove box and handed Paul one of the guns Luther had supplied me with, a stainless steel HK P-7, the gun James Bond had used when Daniel Craig took over the secret agent role.

"He wouldn't be the first Russian you shot," I said.

I phoned Jimmy and gave him the bar's address.

"Where the hell is that?" Strangely, he didn't sound as smashed as I thought he'd be with nothing but a television and an endless supply of dope to keep him company.

"Who cares?" I said. "Get a cab and pay him extra to blatantly disregard any speed limit signs. Get your ass here pronto."

After swinging around the pub six times, I finally settled for a pay lot across the street from the bar. Parking cost me fifteen dollars and for all I knew the Acura would only need to sit in the spot for fifteen minutes, especially if Scarface decided to try to cash in on the bounty Sergei had put out for Paul.

I walked down four flagstone steps and entered the dark dwelling. An L-shaped bar ran along the eastern side of the pub. Framed photographs of famous Irish Americans from Jack Dempsey to JFK adorned the black paneled walls. Paul and Myron had found a booth in the far western corner where they both stared at the scarred oak table between them. Scarface sat at the bar with a few other drinkers, workingmen with button-down, short sleeved shirts bearing name tags.

This was the first genuine working class bar we'd even come close to in Chicago and I could see why

Sergei might be fond of the place, it's location decidedly outside the limits of Wicker Park.

"Stay here." I didn't sit when I reached the booth. I removed my denim coat and laid it on the red vinyl next to Myron. "When Jimmy gets here wave him over then tell him to find a place to sit by the entrance." I glanced over at Scarface who still seemed unaffected by our patronage of the place. "We only make a move if he does. If he walks away, we let him do so and come up with something else."

"What else?" Paul asked.

"Migrating to a South American country would be my first thought." I forced a laugh. If this didn't work we all had serious problems ahead, all of us except maybe Jimmy. But Jimmy would always side with me, so my problems were his.

"I ain't got no passport," Myron said.

"Then I guess you're shit out of luck if Scarface declines our offer." I turned and approached the bar.

I took the stool next to Scarface and was about to speak when I heard a click, a sound six months ago I would have called foreign but that I now knew to be thumb pressing the hammer down on a semi-automatic pistol.

"Bitch boy from horse town." Scarface laughed. "I figure you already done it, fag, but take a look at my lap."

Pointed at me, laying on his thigh, was a .22 Colt Woodsman.

"You Americans always act and then think. I recognize your friend, the one boss wants dead. But I wonder why he come to Chicago. So I wait. Then I see you. Now I am very interested to know what lame brain bullshit that's brought you north."

"I'm Jon." I extended my hand.

Scarface did not accept. He finished his drink and said, "I know."

"I'm not going to waste too much of your time. But I'd like to know what to call you for the sake of civility."

"What makes you think this even has chance of going civil?"

"You haven't opened fire yet."

That got me a smile. "Lex," he said. "Lex. Like bad guy in Superman."

"Luckily we're not going to be discussing going head to head with Superman tonight."

"What were you thinking then?"

"What are you drinking?"

Lex followed me over to the booth. As we sat down, the bell jingled over the front door and Jimmy stumbled inside. Lex reached for his Woodsman where he'd holstered it under his right arm. He could tell Jimmy was one of us and perhaps sensed some sort of setup.

"It's cool." I lightly placed my hands on Lex's biceps. "It's cool. He's just here to talk, like us."

I waved Jimmy over. Lex sat beside Myron and Jimmy slumped down next to Paul, momentarily resting his head on Paul's shoulder.

"Jesus, man." Paul shook Jimmy off of him.

"You guys best get your shit together," Lex said. "I already know where this is going. And I also know you wouldn't have come," Lex looked right at me, "had you not sensed how tired I am of being treated like a retard spider monkey by that little fat man."

"This Russian's pretty goddamn quick on the uptake," Jimmy slurred his words. He'd had another shot after I called him. Mad Dog was right. One day my friend would be a liability. But for tonight, more pressing matters required attendance.

I pulled a chair to the edge of the table and we all huddled our heads closer like football players deciding on a formation.

"You want me help you get rid of boss so you two faggots," Lex pointed at me and then Paul, "can keep carrying on without fear of castration, death, so forth."

"We're really not gay," Paul said.

"Sure." Lex rolled his eyes. "And I never killed a man with an axe before."

"I don't what y'all be talkin' bout." Myron refilled his glass of beer from the pitcher they'd ordered while I parked. He'd gotten a little tipsy, a young man unused to drink. "If this be what Russians act like, I like the motherfuckers."

"You're alright too, my young friend," Lex said to Myron. "You keep mouth shut, ears open, and eyes always on lookout. Wish we had three more of you instead of two gays and doper."

"Try sitting in a car with him for five hours," Paul said.

"Enough of the bickering," I raised my voice only slightly lest someone who knew Sergei and the bounty on Paul enter. I asked Lex, "Do you think it's possible? Replace you with Sergei up here and Myron with Cotton down in Louisville."

201

"Possible?" Lex chewed his lower lip a moment. "Yes. Probable?" Lex spun his head like an owl, appraising briefly each man at the booth. "No."

There was a momentary sense of utter failure and hopelessness that seemed to pervade the booth. Even Lex appeared disappointed that we hadn't a better shot at changing the guards.

Then he surprised us all and said, "But we try anyway. I rather die than kiss that fat cocksuck's ass any longer."

34

WE'D COME TO Chicago on just the right weekend to kill Sergei. According to Lex, the next day the Russian mobster who could stunt double for Danny DeVito would be in Peoria looking at horses and trucks for his blossoming export business. His only protection would be Lex, who had switched over to the Louisville side, and another Lurch lookalike by the name of Max.

"Problem not with taking out Max and Sergei," Lex had told us at the bar. "You see, this is thing we have here in Chicago... it become big mess since mid-90s. For example, if Paul had killed me, Sergei probably not bat an eye. But Ivan was blood. And the way Sergei and his people are about blood... well... there's no pleasant way to put this. We have to kill rest of Sergei's relatives."

"Jesus." Jimmy rested his head on Paul's shoulder again. Paul let him remain, then shook him off, saying, "You need serious help, junky."

"Not like little children or women." Lex tried to reassure Jimmy and Paul who both looked a little green at the gills. "Just Sergei's brother, and his father Uri, perhaps scariest man I've ever met."

We decided it'd be best to take them all out in one fell swoop, not give Sergei's people enough time to even plan retaliation. Jimmy and Myron would take Lex's car and meet him in Peoria to take care of Sergei and the other guard. Sergei's dad and brother had just become another one of mine and Paul's problems. Again, however, good fortune found us through Lex's thin, near-gray lips. "Uri owns bar on North side. He and his sons normally have drinks before opening. Sergei, as I told you, has business elsewhere. So at least your targets will be in one place."

So here were the facts:

There were two targets. They'd be in one locale. And one of them scared Lex who himself scared me worse than herpes.

As if he'd read my mind Lex advised, "It probably be best if you can do this from distance. Don't get close to these two men."

Great, I thought. I'd always wanted to work with explosives.

It turns out the pen is indeed mightier than the sword. Or, for these purposes, the pen and a shitload of C-4 that Lex scored us before he left.

The Friday Sergei took his trip to Peoria turned out to be the same day telephone books were delivered in Chicago. I'd scooped one from the doorway of a bar that didn't open until late, carved a nice rectangle out of the pages as I did when transporting drugs via dictionaries or literature sets. The four Louisville boys stood with the Russian in Jimmy's room at the Ramada Inn a few exits just within the city limits

Lex had molded the C-4 to perfectly fit the square I'd created in the middle of the Yellow Pages with a box cutter. He'd inserted two ink-pen looking detonators into the clay-like substance that, upon dialing a certain cell phone number Lex had rigged, would send a shock wave through the malleable material that would ignite explosion.

"No worry about dropping or accidental blowing up." Lex closed the dictionary and offered it to me. "Only shock wave can detonate."

I accepted the telephone book wearily. Right as my hands touched the yellow spine, Jimmy, thinking he was funny, stomped on the floor next to the bed.

I flinched and shivered then saw Jimmy laying on the bed, embracing his small beer gut as he laughed himself half-sober at the joke he'd played.

Lex handed me a matchbook. Inside he'd written the number to dial to set off the detonator.

"Do not mistake number for girlfriend's," Lex said. "Last booty call you'll ever make."

Everyone had turned into a comedian since the Louisville boys had come to town.

35

LEX TOLD US that Sergei's father owned the entire walk-up out of which the gangster's brother, Karl, and their father operated the family bar, Uri's.

"Don't worry about... how your American military say it... collateral damage." Lex had assured me and Paul in the parking lot of the Ramada as we prepared for battle. Myron had almost prematurely ejaculated when Uri handed him the pistol to use in their showdown in Peoria. The kid sat in the passenger seat of Lex's Lexus ejecting the clip, slamming it home, thumbing the hammer down, counting the bullets while the grown ups talked. "The buildings next to bar all abandoned. And the upstairs of Uri's is where old man lives. This part of plan hard to fuck up, but I'm sure you two could manage."

"Thanks for the vote of confidence." Paul walked around to the driver's side of the Acura. Implicit in him taking the wheel was the unspoken agreement that I'd be stuck with the job of handling the explosion.

I let it go.

Paul had done enough killing for a little while. And he hadn't mentioned his failure to reform Myron, the very reason he'd shot down those men in Bardstown. All he'd said of the subject was, "At least he'll be a king."

We'd timed it so, with any luck, Myron and Lex would

take out Sergei within minutes of the downtown explosion I was to trigger. Luckily, this job didn't involve intense surveillance as Lex had emphasized that the bar would be deserted until four. I'd already ran across the sunny, abandoned Chicago street to switch out the phone books. When I entered the Acura I took several deep breaths.

"What's wrong with you?" Paul asked. "Have you been dabbling into guided mediation and forgot to mention it?"

I wiped the sweat from my brow with my forearm. The river breeze had done little to lower the humidity and I'd removed my dress shirt, wearing only a plain white tee and camouflage shorts Irina had bought me at a thrift store years back. I held off on responding to Paul and removed my cell phone from my shorts pocket.

"And you're sweating like you're going through withdrawal again," Paul continued giving me grief.

"I didn't notice you offering to carry around the C-4 explosives."

"Ahh, get over it. Lex said even fire couldn't make that thing go off. You have to dial the number."

Oh no, I thought. The phone number.

"Shit." I grabbed my discarded dress shirt from the backseat and checked the pockets. Then I checked my shorts.

"Don't tell me." Paul punched the wheel. "Don't even say it out loud."

"I lost the number." I fully expected to get punched but instead Paul ordered me to help him toss the Acura, search every inch of it until we found the matchbook that contained the phone number. "Lex told us not to call him. He was pretty serious."

Sergei had gotten paranoid since he lost his nephew. Any strange phone calls he overheard Lex receiving could be the end of our new scarfaced friend. And with Lex would die any hopes of our survival.

"We have no choice." Paul got out of the car. "We have to find it. That or we improvise."

"Improvise?" I said.

Paul and I got down on our knees, suffering the hot pavement of Chicago summer as we reached under the seats and lifted the floor mats. At that very moment, Myron was driving Lex's sports car to Peoria to help ambush the most ruthless Chicago gangster in recent history. He and Jimmy were probably arguing over which radio station to tune into, or which Kentucky basketball teams they supported, but at least they had air conditioning and weren't responsible for enough explosives to level a three-story building.

Lucky bastards, I thought.

Paul began kicking the side of the rented Acura. We'd torn the interior apart looking for the book and all we'd found was a box of tampons some cheating housewife had likely bought. Paul tossed the tampons in the middle of the street.

"We're dead men." Paul slumped on his side, resting on the hood of the car. Paul faced north up the downtown side street. He wouldn't even look at me. "I suppose when they show up we just run in blasting, pray that we've become good enough shots to walk out alive."

We both knew the outcome of a gunfight with Uri

and his son. Lex had explained to us that before Uri had immigrated to the U.S.A., he'd served as a sniper, killing nearly three dozen of the Taliban, kind of like Luther's goons, Kelly and Cletus.

"Old man can still throw a quarter in the air and shoot a hole through it," Lex said when we had brought up the idea of storming Uri's, guns blazing. "He keeps a loaded pistol within arms reach of anywhere he could be standing in bar. Karl also great shot. Not as good as father, but good enough to take all four of us out before we had chance to draw."

A gunfight with Uri and Karl was suicide. But we couldn't walk away now.

"I guess we better lock and load and position ourselves or whatever." Paul pushed himself from the hood of the Acura. He looked like a defeated, broken man if I've ever seen one. I too believed all hope was lost. That all the carnage, bloodshed, lies, and general criminality were all for nothing.

Then I remembered the most likely place a complete idiot would stick the matchbook Lex had given me.

The good news was I knew now where I'd hidden the matchbook.

"Now hit me with the bad news." Paul stood with his feet shoulder length apart as if preparing for the first blow from a formidable street fighting opponent.

"I stuck it in the phone book."

We both stared at the bar's entrance, at the red brick and tinted windows, at the phone book that I'd left on the flagstone stoop.

36

THE CLOCK IN the Acura read three twenty p.m. I could only pray that I had enough time to grab the matchbook from the phone book and run back to the car before Uri and Karl arrived for their pre-shift drinks.

"What should I do if they show up and catch you red handed?" Paul asked, hunching down in the driver's seat of the Acura, talking to me through the open window.

"Wait until I do something." I shrugged, unsure of my own answer. "I'll try to play it off."

"How?" Paul said.

"Feel like we're wasting a lot of time here. I could have had the matchbook by now."

"Okay. Fine. Go. Hurry."

I'd never run so fast in my life. The struggle to catch my breath once I reached the sidewalk in front of Uri's made me ashamed of how I'd let myself go. I examined my abdomen. There wasn't any real fat, but nor was there any muscle. Laying around high for years will make mush of a man's body.

Then I caught my breath, caught site of the phone book and remembered that I had matters at hand more pressing than my figure.

I opened the book to the cutout where Lex had fashioned the plastic. I flipped the pages that came before the explosives and out fell the matchbook. I thanked God who all cowards turn to when facing the reaper. When I turned to run back to the car, two men stood before me, matching quizzical expressions on both their pallid faces. Like the other Russians we'd met, besides of course the well fed Sergei, these men looked extremely vitamin depleted and in need of serious nutritional advice.

Before either spoke, I knew I was looking at Uri and Karl.

I had some explaining to do.

Luckily, I'd shut the phone book and placed it back on the stoop before turning and discovering the Russians. They didn't know my intentions which Uri, the half-dead looking chap in the London Fog blazer and scally cap, said in so many words: "Who fuck are you? Why you standing around in front of my place?"

Serendipity intervened. Karl answered for me. He came up with a better excuse than I ever could have under such pressure. "Papa." Karl lightly wrapped his fingers around his father's wrist. "He Yellow Pages man. He just dropping off phone book." Then Karl slapped me hard on the shoulder.

I wondered if all Russians had such issues with personal boundaries

Uri looked at me. Uri looked at the phone book.

Then Uri broke a smile, wiped his brow and squinted at the sun behind me. "Sounds like shit job."

"Yes, sir." I walked briskly across the street and around the corner where we'd parked the Acura. Without even checking over my shoulder to see if the father or son had discovered what lay within their copy of the Chicago Yellow Pages, I removed my cell and dialed the number Lex had written inside the matchbook.

Paul was rolling down his window wearing the same panic on his face that was there ninety percent of the time since he became a fixture at the bookstore. I didn't think anything of it as I reached the passenger side of the Acura and hit send on the burner cell phone.

Lex told us it would take a few seconds for the phone to signal the shock wave.

Paul kept pointing at the bar, yelling something. The passenger window was still rolled up so I couldn't make out his words.

Then I looked back for the brief moment before the bar turned into three giant balls of fire and saw the old man walking his dog out front.

37

FORTUNE'S WHEEL LANDED more favorably on our boys in Peoria.

Lex told me and Paul that he'd offered to handle driving duties for the day, not an unusual occurrence in their crew's daily workings. This involved some bickering between Lex and Max which only served to amuse Sergei. Lex then faked car trouble at a rest stop just north of Peoria. Max, a former mechanic, asked Lex to pop the hood and got out of the car to check the engine. As Lex predicted, Sergei, who possessed the patience of a crack baby, got out of the back seat after allowing Max less than five minutes to examine the vehicle's mechanics. While Sergei yelled, Jimmy and Myron stepped from the grove of trees next to where Lex had parked. Myron shot Sergei twice in the back of the head. Max drew his piece. Jimmy had the drop on him but his automatic jammed. Max smiled, probably thinking Lex had his back and would take care of the black kid while he did the white guy who dressed like a homeless person.

Lex had stepped behind Max, but not to assist.
Lex and Myron dragged the bodies behind the grove, left the Tahoe in the rest stop parking lot, and headed back to Chicago in Lex's Lexus.

"Mission still accomplished." Lex raised his glass.

"Here's to my new American partners. I have feeling you will treat me better than that dead fuck Sergei ever consider."

We'd met at another Irish pub that Lex favored called Galway Bay. "I like the Irish," Lex said. "They almost as mean as Russians." I could attest to that, my father a second generation Scotch-Irishman who would break a man's nose who admittedly voted anything but Democrat. The inside of Lex's second favorite pub was nearly identical to the bar where Lex had initially agreed to betray his employer. Paul and I slowly raised our glasses to meet Sergei's. We hadn't said a word since we left the rubble that had been Uri's. There was nothing left of the old man and his dog. They'd been standing close enough to the initial blast, Lex had explained, that there probably weren't even solid limbs left to put together for police to identify.

"Collateral damage." Sergei turned his palms upward, the universal "what are you gonna do?" sign.

"You said there wouldn't be any collateral damage." Paul's voice was horse and gravelly from trying to scream and warn me about the old man.

"Are we going to cry all day or celebrate?" Lex asked.

"I mean at least it was an old dude." Jimmy's condition, morally, physically, spiritually, was on a steep decline. The first thing he'd done when he entered the bar was make a b-line for the bathroom. When he'd walked back out, he'd done the dope fiend lean against the bar for a good minute before Paul stood up and escorted him back to the booth. "What?" Jimmy asked when he caught the disdainful glare Paul had fixed on the felonious addict.

"Why are you looking at me like that? I'm simply saying at least it wasn't a kid or a baby or..."

"Honestly." Lex, for the first time since I'd laid eyes on him, appeared genuinely disturbed. "I feel worse about dog."

"I know what you mean." The words left my mouth before my brain could form a filter to stop them.

"So we're supposed to just shrug this off like we did with what happened in Cincinnati?" Paul's eyelids fluttered in repudiation. He was visibly disgusted at the rest of the table's willingness to write off the old man's death as the cost of doing business.

The cost of doing business.

That's how Jimmy put it.

The factors you couldn't control when pulling a job, when living the life we'd half-thoughtfully chosen. A teenage boy shot to death on a Midwestern ghetto street. An old man and his little dog blown to bits. This was now my life. Could I live with these things? Could I accept collateral damage as the cost of the good life, if you could call it that?

I offered another toast, this one to the old man and his dog, and as I pulled my Diet Coke back for a sip, I said loudly, "Now, we never bring it up again."

38

LOUISVILLE NEVER LOOKED so good.

After dropping the boys off at the Walgreens parking lot in the Highlands where they'd left their cars, I headed east to Anchorage, where the other half lives, them and Luther James Longmire. I'd checked the papers that morning and the Chicago Police wrote off the clearly related murders downtown and south in Peoria to a rival mafia, the Italians, Irish, or another sect of Russians. Luther had likely gotten word of the slayings, and I was sweating through my T-shirt and denim coat, fearing facing my boss with the truth of what I'd been up to over the last week.

I wish I'd listened to Mad Dog more about watching obsessively for tails. Maybe I would've seen the Mercedes following me all the way from the bookstore, which I found empty when I stopped there to change clothes since it was closer from Walgreens than my apartment

Amara should have been watching the place. And I should have found it strange that she wasn't and that I hadn't gotten a call explaining her absence.

When I arrived in Anchorage, all was revealed. I had planned to take a cab back to the store since Luther had rented me the Acura. I'd explained that the Alero's AC was out and a road trip to New York would be murder without the comfort.

I simply didn't want to take my own car to a slaughter.

I could have easily gotten a fake ID and rented a car myself. Another one of those "what if's" that will haunt me the rest of my life. What if I hadn't been forced to travel to east Louisville to return Luther's rented vehicle that day? Would enough time have elapsed for the smite of the email he'd discovered—I'd warned Amara not to contact me in writing—to pass?

I doubt it.

But maybe Irina wouldn't have been spying on the bookstore the day I chose to drive out and face Luther.

I still hadn't noticed the Mercedes, which Irina had parked off to the side of the country road where Luther lived, when I pulled into the long driveway and parked behind the Rolls Luther had bought Amara for her last birthday. I traipsed up the front porch steps of the massive yellow gabled mansion and rang the doorbell.

"Come on in." Luther's voice echoed through the antechamber that led to the rest of the house.

Amara sat at the end of the long dining room table smiling. I'll never forget the malice that permeated from her closed, curled lips. "I'd say I'm sorry but I wouldn't mean it much. You would've done the same to me."

I turned and standing in the kitchen doorway stood Luther, on either side of him the two ex-Marines who'd followed us to Cincinnati, Kelly and Cletus. I almost didn't recognize them without Kevlar and camouflage. Their street clothes though still had a paramilitary air, logo-less T-shirts tucked into cargo pants. They both had automatic pistols in holsters clipped to their belts.

I hadn't even brought my gun, predicting how frivolous armament would turn out under Luther's roof.

"You try to take my woman." Luther threw the internet print out of the Chicago Post's front page on the table. "Then you try to take my business."

"Luther..." I searched for the words and stuttered on his name a few times before offering pathetically, "It's not how it seems. I thought... I thought..."

I hadn't had the wind knocked out of me since grade school when a little no-neck monster named Calvin Groves tossed a basketball full force into my solar plexus to get a laugh from the other popular kids. When Luther drove his fist into the same spot, that old elementary school memory flooded back for a moment, then I had to focus all energy and attention on trying, and failing for almost a full minute, to breath.

"You went behind my back." Luther towered over me, pointing, castigating. "Does that sound about right?"

"I was trying..." I took my second deep breath in over sixty seconds. "I was trying to maintain."

"Maintain?" Luther laughed. He removed his cowboy hat and sat at the end of the table opposite Amara, his foot an inch from my face. "The language of a junkie."

"I'm telling you..." Tears were streaming down my cheeks as I struggled to speak. "I was trying to get us a man in.... a man who'd be beholden to us running the West End."

Luther laughed harder.

"And in one fell swoop," I continued, "save Paul and get us a better foothold in Chicago. I'm sorry, Luther. Paul's my partner. I couldn't do him that way."

Luther laughed some more. "And you was gonna hand all this to me on a silver platter, I suppose? I guess that was your way of repaying me for sleeping with my woman."

"She's your fucking cousin," I yelled.

"That's right." He pointed at Amara, still keeping eyes with me. "She's my blood. That's why I'm gonna forgive her. And that's why she told me, after getting to know you real well, that you'd never play second fiddle to no one for very long. That's why she sniffed you out. Had to get close to you. She didn't give two shits about you, son. It was all business. And maybe, just maybe, she was killing a little boredom off too."

"He'll take you out the way he handled the Russians." Amara smiled wider, talking to Luther explicitly now. "Just like he was going to leave me for that little rich bitch."

"What?" I asked, rising to my knees to look at Amara.

Luther pressed his boot heel to my chest and forced me back down on my side. "I like you right where you are. When I want you on your knees, you'll know it."

"I followed you. I saw you bring her that money. I saw the way you looked at her," Amara screamed. I'd never heard a sound like the wail she let out aside from in B-slasher movies.

"I haven't seen her in weeks," I yelled back, my voice breaking like a teenager in the midst of growing pains. "And that was before I ever even touched you."

Amara shot out of her chair and crossed the room to stand next to Luther and stare down at me. The two Longmires' sneers matched and betrayed their kinship.

"It doesn't matter anyway. Like my cousin said, family comes first. And I don't believe for a second you wouldn't have turned a gun on Luther the first opportunity you saw. Then you'd have tossed me to the side for that little trust fund cunt."

"I bet a lot of people told you when you were growing up, 'You're too smart for your own good.'" Luther stood next to his cousin and lover. He held her hand. "But I bet none of them thought you'd end up like this. Maybe rehab. A few misdemeanors. If your guidance counselors could only see you now, golden boy."

I heard the creak of the front door opening. No one else seemed to notice. But when I turned my face to the entrance that led to Luther's foyer, Irina stood in her cut-off jeans and a denim shirt, her purse slung around her shoulder, her long roan hair, my weakness, tied in a pony tail. She was wearing the same outfit the first time I saw her.

"That's the bitch." Amara reached inside Luther's coat and removed his long .357 Magnum.

Then Amara killed the woman who loved me enough to stalk me and research candidly what kind of trouble I'd caused for myself.

39

I WEPT FROM the moment Irina hit the floor until the two ex-Marines dragged me kicking and screaming out to the trunk of Luther's El Dorado where they locked me alone for a few moments. The trunk lid then opened again and they dropped Irina's body in with me.

I held her the entire ride.

I don't know exactly how long the drive to the Portland docks takes from Anchorage but I lost myself in the trunk darkness, in Irina's matted, bloody hair. I stroked her long locks hundreds of times, a period at the end of which my knuckle scraped against the compartment which held the tools included with the car in case of a breakdown.

"I'll be right back, baby," I told Irina, then began clawing at the cheap cloth interior until I'd gotten the compartment unlatched enough to reach inside.

I commenced holding Irina, placing the tire iron between our bodies, hers turning colder with each mile.

The car stopped. I didn't know where we were yet, but I knew that unless fate intervened or the tire iron was sufficient against two trained Marines, I'd be meeting with Irina again soon, or not, depending on what lay beyond death's veil.

I heard the key enter the trunk lock, then loud voices, Kelly and Cletus arguing about something.

Then I heard Mad Dog say, "Step away from the trunk."

"We're doing our jobs," Cletus yelled.

"I've seen Luther in this mode," Mad Dog said. "That's why I drove out there today to see if there were any reasoning with him. I heard the shots, waited, and sure enough, I got proof right here that he's already off the reservation. Only difference is, last time he pulled a Richard III and killed every member of his own crew, I wasn't part of it. I've already shaken you two tailing me twice over the last few days, probably since that crazy cooze of his turned on Catlett."

"We were just following orders." The sense of defeat mixed with resignation in Cletus's voice told me that Mad Dog had the drop on them. He'd either made it clear that he was close to drawing or already had his gun out.

"You never thought about why he had you tailing me?" Mad Dog asked.

I covered Irina's ears. I knew what was coming.

"I might buy that from you, Cletus, considering you got the IQ of a halfwit chimp. But Kelly, you know what happens to ninety percent of the people Luther has tailed. You were probably already planning a setup, something to impress the old man with, a way to get rid of a police officer that would never draw any attention to Luther James Longmire."

"Don't." The voice was so hoarse, pleading, and pathetic, I couldn't tell if it belonged to Kelly or Cletus.

The gunshots I placed. A high-caliber semi-automatic pistol with a suppressor fixed to the barrel.

Ah, the things I'd learned since I'd killed Carter Parrant.

The dim light of evening blazed in as the trunk opened. The sunrays harshly contrasted the pitch-black that had immersed me since Anchorage. I covered my eyes. As I slowly removed my hands and adjusted my sight to the sunshine that had blinded me moments ago, all I remember seeing was red. My hands. My shirt. I'd killed men. I'd stood by while others were murdered, a close-mouthed accomplice. But I'd never had this much blood on my body or clothes in my life.

I fell out of the trunk screaming, tearing my shirt off, unbuckling my pants.

It took Mad Dog about two minutes of slapping me around to force me out of my state.

"Pull your damn pants up," Mad Dog said. "Jesus."

I assumed since he hadn't shot me yet, since he'd in fact saved me from a riverbed grave, and since his piece was now holstered, that Mad Dog was now an ally.

He let me weep for a minute then shook me. "We have business to attend to. Those two morons I just dealt with are not Luther's only operators. He's got men looking for us all over the city. We've got to move, and quickly. Now help me with these bodies. I brought some blocks and chains."

"Not her," I said. "We're not putting her in the river."

"By all that's holy." Mad Dog dropped Cletus's feet back into the silt. He'd been waiting for me to help him lift the corpse.

"We're leaving her here," I said. "Someone needs to find her. Her family deserves to know what happened. She was innocent."

"If she knew you, I highly doubt that." Mad Dog

winced. I could tell he'd regretted opening such a fresh wound. "Fine. We leave her. But we toss these two."

After chaining the bodies to the cinder blocks we paddled out to the middle of the river in an old abandoned boat we'd found tied to the docks. I was half afraid the thing would sink on us, but it made it halfway across the Ohio where we threw Cletus and Kelly over. The evening dark had come and the River was empty of motor-skiers or fathers and sons fishing. The brisk winds, a hint of Fall's arrival, probably kept many water sport enthusiasts at bay. That or, it being a Wednesday night, people were just too damn busy with normal life, all signs of which had now become foreign to me.

We'd decided to leave Irina in the trunk of Luther's El Dorado along with the Magnum Amara had used to kill her. Both Luther's and Amara's prints would be found on the piece. This would jam Luther up with the LMPD enough to force him to go on the run for a bit, maybe to one of his farms he had no legal attachment to, all ran under LLCs created in the name of a paid-off mountain relative.

Luther would panic and start moving all his dope to a new spot. Probably let his migrant works and Eastern Kentucky hillbillies help him load the bricks of heroin before he killed them too.

"He's a big stickler for loose ends," Mad Dog said.

"Then like I told Paul, when he warned me about this day coming..." I slammed the trunk on Irina. I'd hear that sound until the day someone did the same to me, probably in a similar scenario, left for police to find or thrown into the river wrapped in chains. "We need to

224

act first. We've got you, me, Paul, Jimmy, and Myron if he wants to get involved."

"About that." Mad Dog hung his head, wouldn't move his gaze from the silt and mud at our feet.

I closed my eyes.

I could tell he had news he didn't want to deliver and I had a premonition as to its nature.

Luther had already taken out one of my friends.

40

UNFORTUNATELY FOR LUTHER, according to Mad Dog's view of the day's events, the two idiotic Marines had botched the killing of Jimmy O'Hearn. Rather than catch him in some dark alley, do him, and sink him in acid or lye, they simply pulled a drive-by as Jimmy was closing his mom's garage door. He was probably taking her Jeep Grand Cherokee to go and find a fix.

When the truck pulled up in the drive and, as Jimmy described to Mad Dog, first on the scene since he'd been keeping an angelic eye on all of us, Kelly and Cletus lookalikes, older and worse for wear than the first two gun men of Luther's we'd met, Jimmy, upon seeing the killers with their guns drawn, simply removed his sunglasses, placed his wallet on the hood, and asked them if they'd avoid the face.

They agreed.

They fired both of their Uzis into Jimmy's chest, leaving his entrails spilling, and for his mom to find, having come home early, spooking the killers into fleeing before loading Jimmy's body for disposal. Jimmy was still alive and got to tell his mother he was sorry for being a shit junkie son and that he loved her. Then Mad Dog showed and got the whole story from my loyal near-dead friend.

Mad Dog owned property in the south end that, according to the dirty cop, was unknown to any other police or gun thugs on Luther's payroll. "The mortgage is under my ex-wife's name," Mad Dog said. "I have to pay the bitch a grand every month to keep her mouth shut. But trust me, if I ever met a soul on this earth as cold-blooded and hard as Luther, it's my ex, Jenny. No one would think to talk to her given the deep-seeded hatred between me and that cruel, cruel woman."

The shotgun shack on Southland Drive sat in the middle of the Iriquois neighborhood, adjacent to four different sets of housing projects. The house was virtually unfurnished. A few wicker back chairs and a sagging coffee table made up the living room furniture but the kitchen and bedrooms were empty. Mad Dog had brought a few sleeping bags that he tossed in the corner of the living room where we now sat, processing and plotting.

"You think he got Paul too?" I asked.

"Don't know." Mad Dog set two cups of coffee on the wobbly table. "Haven't been able to reach him since I found you. He was still breathing last time I checked. He make sure his people are safe?"

"His son's out of the state," I said.

"That'll do for now," Mad Dog said.

I took a long drink of coffee. For some reason the caffeine had the opposite effect it's known for; the drink calmed my nerves. We'd stopped at a Texaco for me to wash my hands and face and Mad Dog bought me a black T-shirt in the gift shop that read "Pretty Women Make Me Buy Beer. Ugly Women make me drink beer."

I thanked him sincerely.

As for the blood on my pants, Mad Dog kept a few changes of clothes at his safe house and let me borrow one of his token pair of black slacks that barely fit me. Had Mad Dog not had a belt, the slacks would've fallen down constantly.

"At least you don't look like the living dead," he'd said after I finished dressing in the bathroom.

"We've got to find Paul." I rubbed my temple, shock still pervading every inch of my body and bowels. "We can't pull this off, just the two of us"

"Myron is gonna sit this one out." Mad Dog finished his coffee. "It's lose lose for him. He's best in hiding right now. If he gets killed during our attack we gotta find a new king of the west. If we get killed in the attack, he better flee the fucking country."

"He doesn't have a passport."

"Well, maybe Timbuktu will do for him. The point is. It's me and you... and Paul if he shows."

"What are we even talking about?"

"Don't be thick, kid."

"What about Paul, then?"

"You must have left your phone at Luther's because he ain't been able to reach you. But when he heard about Jimmy, he bit the bullet and called me. He asked which side I was on. I told him."

"So how long has it been since you've spoken to Paul?" I began pacing the room, sadly, like Paul would in such a situation.

"A few hours ago."

"Jesus." I yelled. "Why didn't you say so?"

"You never asked. And I think he wanted to feel me out. Be sure I was on his and your side."

"What side are you on?"

"Gee, let me think? A psychopathic redneck that's cleaning house so he can hire a new crew and not worry about any of us trying to take over or rolling when the cops get hold of one of us OR the man who planned every intelligent move we've made to build this thing."

"Strange bedfellows." I finished my coffee and stood. "I didn't get an answer about Paul."

"He knows where we are right now. If he shows he's alive. If not, well..." Mad Dog knelt and removed a few loose boards from the living room floor. He reached in the dark makeshift cubbyhole and brought out a massive duffel bag. He unzipped and tilted it toward me.

The bag was filled to the brim with a plethora of guns, AR-15s, Glocks, and bulletproof vests.

"If I'm right," Mad Dog said. "Luther's loading up his trucks and fleeing Kentucky, using those Mexicans to get the horses in the trailers and the heroin taped under the wheel wells. If we're lucky, he's still hard at work and we can hit him hard while he's distracted."

"What are we gonna do?"

"Like you said, 'act first.'" Mad Dog began fastening the Velcro of the Kevlar vest he'd dug out of the weapons bag. He then holstered a revolver on his hip and chose a Mossberg shotgun. He racked the pump, leaned down to the bag again, and began loading shells. "Technically, though. Luther has acted first. He tried to kill all of us and was successful with Jimmy. But the kind of 'act first'

I'm talking about is much more extreme."

"And why is that?" I leaned down and began rummaging through the gun bag. I chose Kevlar and a shotgun, mimicking Mad Dog. "We're going to kill all of them, aren't we?"

"If you wish to live the rest of your life, yes."

I grabbed a HK-P7 with a holster which I clipped to my belt. "I'm okay with that. Luther and that sick twist took the only thing I love."

"Which one? Amara or the one before her."

"Amara ain't the Amara she pretended to be. I loved Irina the way you're supposed to love someone. The relationship wasn't filled with deception and subterfuge."

"Now you're the one avoiding questions." Mad Dog lay his shotgun on the coffee table and finished his coffee. "What are you gonna do about Amara if you see her there?"

"I honestly don't know yet."

41

PAUL ARRIVED HALF an hour later, hung over, but relieved to see me alive. He looked like a street person with his toboggan and undershirt, jeans ripped at the crotch and knees. He must have gone off the radar in a rush when he heard about Jimmy, no time to pack or make any kind of arrangements to leave town, probably praying that Mad Dog and I had a plan.

"When I tried to call your phone, Luther answered," Paul said. "He told me that I better make arrangements for my funeral or cremation if that was my thing. Then he hung up. I didn't know if you had any chance of surviving until Mad Dog called and said he'd make sure you made it through the night." Paul lightly patted Mad Dog's wrist. I was surprised the cop didn't punch Paul. Instead the ancient killer nodded, clearly humbled by the danger we all faced.

"At least we ain't alone now," Paul said.

Mad Dog, in a rare act of mercy, ran down the street to a gas station to get Paul some coffee and aspirin to help the hungover malcontent get his head clear.

I explained our plan to Paul, knowing he'd go along, begrudgingly, considering his son's life was at stake.

"There's a good chance we won't survive this." Paul rubbed his eyes then his temple. "How many men has he got working the farm?"

231

"I've only been there once," I said. "Ten or fifteen if I had to guess."

"Are they all armed?"

"I don't know. I do know that Luther's fixing to leave town and has men all over the city looking for us," I said. "But if he dies, they'll know they won't get paid and they will stop. It's that simple."

"Why'd you have to fuck that nutjob cousin of his?" Paul asked me in a straightforward tone, no real anger or resentment to be detected. He just wanted to know why someone with a decent-sized IQ like me could fumble so grandly.

"You're correct that that was a bad move on my part. But to be honest, I think this day would come no matter what. Mad Dog says that Luther goes through periods of intense paranoia every few years and offs a good portion of his crew, just in case there's a rat or someone with ideas of taking over."

"We really don't have a choice, do we?" Paul was accepting what had to be done. It always took him longer than the rest of us, probably because, when you get right down to it, the guy had a heart and truly wanted to be a decent human being, if not for himself, for his son.

"They killed Irina," I said. "And I don't think he'd hesitate to hurt your son. Is Adam still safe?"

"No way Luther could find him anytime soon. Not in fucking Iowa. Given long enough, he may be able to track him down. I have no family in town for him to question or torture, the sick bastard."

"Paul." Mad Dog leaned over him, a coach ready to give a half-decent pep talk before the big game. "We have no choice. If I were you I'd wash up. Then I'd dig through that gun bag and get ready."

42

MAD DOG STARED at the weapons he'd laid out on the table, those he and I had not already claimed. Paul wanted the AR-15. He'd fallen in love with the craftsmanship integral to the machine gun's structure.

"You have no idea how to fire a machine gun," Mad Dog told him. "You need to choose a few pistols and stick to what you know."

"How hard can it be?" Paul held the massive weapon, aiming out the back window.

Mad Dog rolled his eyes. "I understand the temptation, Paul. But we're looking to win this thing, not pretend we're in some shitty Schwarzenegger film."

"Okay," Paul laid the gun back on the table. "What is so difficult about handling this beautiful piece of American firepower?"

"First of all, shut up." Mad Dog lightly rubbed the machine gun from barrel to stock as if petting a puppy. "It kicks like hell and it's easy to lose control of your aim. You pull the trigger and the thing just sprays. The only situation where it's essential to carry a piece like this is when you're dealing with a shitload of bastards coming at you in a hoard. Then it's just spray and pray. Point the gun in their direction and unload."

"Ok." Paul laid his hand on the AR-15. "I can set it to semi auto, correct? Fire one bullet at a time. What if I do

234

that until I get in a situation where it's spray and pray?"

"Fine." Mad Dog walked into the living room for his car keys. "But it's on you if you open fire and the gun flies out of your hand, leaving you fucked."

Paul picked up the only other gun on the table, a .38 revolver.

"Then I'll bring this too," Paul told Mad Dog. "Happy?"

The ride to Luther's farm took half an hour. None of us spoke. We all knew this might be the last day of our lives.

We parked Mad Dog's civilian Crowne Vic, a U-Haul affixed to the back, about half a mile away and squatted as we walked through the weeds that surrounded the farm.

There were two guards at the gate. Mad Dog had anticipated this.

"Wait here." Mad Dog crawled to the locked gate where the two sentries stood. When he'd reached the end of the weeds, he drew his pistol from his side holster, affixed a suppressor, took his time to aim, and took them both down within seconds, each head shots.

Mad Dog motioned for us to join him. He reached in the backpack he'd brought and handed both Paul and me wire cutters. He ordered Paul to move in from the left side and me the right. Mad Dog would shoot off the gate's lock, walk straight in, and draw the attention of Luther's killers.

Our job was to lay down fire and take out the men who came for Mad Dog.

I hid behind a rusty, broken down flat bed Ford. Anyone who ran past that didn't fit Mad Dog's or Paul's description, I let loose two blasts from the Mossberg, sometimes decapitating the men completely. I heard the radio Mad Dog had given me buzz, clicked the button on the left of the device and answered, "What?"

"They've got to be in the main storage unit to the north of the property." I heard two or three bursts of machine gun fire then four loud reports from Mad Dog's shotgun. "I'll meet you there."

"What about Paul?"

"He hasn't been answering."

Hardly any of Luther's men were packing automatic weapons. Coming from Hazard, I understood the hillbilly shotgun affinity. That meant the sound of machine gun fire to my left assured me that Paul was alive, just too busy to cease fire and answer his radio.

I clenched my fists and began punching the rusty driver's side door of the old Ford I'd been using as cover. I didn't want to lose another friend. Not because a series of events that, ultimately, I'd set in motion. There was no way to tell Paul where to meet me, that I was ready to end this and leave here with Luther's dope and the money he'd brought for his escape from Kentucky.

I walked slowly past the ramshackle barns. Luther's farm didn't look like much, especially since my only two friends and I had turned it into a slaughterhouse. The land was surrounded by three warehouses forming a triangle around the fenced-in pastures peppered with stacks of hay and water troughs. The buildings were ostensibly stocked with tools, feed, and supplies for the oddly sparse population of animals that roamed the property.

"I'm going to find Luther," I said into the radio, dialing Mad Dog's frequency.

"Don't do that. That place is crawling with armed Mexicans and inbred members of Luther's extended family."

"Then you meet me there and we'll take them together."

"Damnit, kid. Do you ever listen?"

"You forget. Sergei hooked us up with a shitload of C-4."

Which is exactly how we leveled the playing field when we reached Luther's main storage warehouse.

After the blast, Mad Dog and I ran in firing, shooting anything that moved. As the smoke cleared, we both saw that we'd already decimated a good half of Luther's guards. A few had hidden behind crates of heroin and were taking pot shots at us. Mad Dog pivoted left. I sprinted right toward the steps that led to Luther's office.

As I racked a fresh rond into the Mossberg, I pulled focus on two bodies at my feet. These dead seemed out of place at first glance. They weren't hillbilly truckers. The two Mexicans in work boots and coveralls had been part of the lowest wrung of Longmire's corporate ladder. Longmire would threaten the daughters, wives and sons of these illegals at the slightest sign of disobedience. If the boss grew sufficiently dissatisfied, the illegal in question would disappear and his former employer would have his way with the poor man's wife and daughter. He'd then sell them for almost nothing to the late Tyrone Cotton. If the dead worker had a son, the boy would be killed just like his father.

Mad Dog had confessed all this about Luther just two hours ago, likely trying to assuage any guilt Paul and I might have felt about killing a whole lot of people

Thinking of Longmire's dead removed all of my hesitation to help him join them. My quarry currently hid behind the second story tin structure that resembled vaguely a double-wide trailer, in keeping with Longmire's hillbilly raising. The bastard was infamously cheap. When designing his ranch, he'd likely chosen the least costly material at hand, abjectly neglecting the safety of his workers. I'd sat on the third to last step, leaning against the stairwell's wrought iron railing to breath and consider what I hoped would be my last murder. Then I remembered that there might be two behind that door.

What to do with the girl if she's in there with Longmire?

Sparks broke across the holey iron steps. I caught only a glimpse of the muzzle flashes pointed upward as I huddled against the locked door. Reinforced steel plates covered the last quarter of the stairwell between the steps and the rail. The rest of the stairs would leave me naked to shooters. I'd been lucky the last survivors hadn't spotted me until I'd drawn near striking distance of my target.

"Looks like someone uprooted your well-laid plans again, Jon." Longmire sounded his Appalachian cackle.

"I'm assuming you can't shoot through the door," I yelled after another round of Uzi fire from below. "You'd have done it by now, otherwise."

"One of them boys are gonna wind up rushing you here in lil' bit. Figure I'll just wait and enjoy the show."

"Why don't you come on out here and get a better

view? Bring Amara with you if she's in there. I'd love to catch up."

The truth was, Longmire and I were both biding time. A psychotic punk rocker and a dirty cop were waiting somewhere in the wings, hopefully aware of that I'd been pinned down and planning immediate extraction.

At least I hoped Paul was still among us.

We three had a common goal, to leave the farm alive with Longmire very dead. As far as I knew, Paul and Milligan were still alive. Longmire's hillbilly army had been vastly decimated and his Mexican indentured servants were nowhere near as loyal. Many had simply fled at the sound of gunfire. This had all gone better than I could have hoped. Until now of course, with me pinned down under machine gun flares. I tried my radio but couldn't hear anything because of the shooting.

I had to pray that I could count on my bedraggled cohorts to take out the gun thugs below before Longmire's "someone" made it to the bottom mouth of the iron stairwell to riddle me with hollow points, only one of which could remove a sufficiently lethal chunk of meat, marrow, bone and muscle.

Longmire and my ex-mistress would then get to watch me die.

This outcome was not acceptable to me.

"Come in and see me, Jon." Longmire's voice turned slightly sterner, a tone I found ridiculous, followed by a far more nerve-racking sound, a round racked into the chamber of a shotgun.

"Me or us?" I yelled after another series of shots and sparks. "Is she in there?"

"Why don't you come in and find out?"

As I listened to footsteps clattering across the cement floor below, drawing closer to the bottom of the stairs, I considered Longmire's offer.

"I just might do that." I put off the decision a few moments longer

43

THROUGHOUT MY VERBAL jousting with Luther, I'd neglected to tell him the small piece of C-4 Mad Dog had handed me before we parted ways. The explosive looked like a clay ball small enough to fit a three year-old's palm.

"It's enough to demolish the asshole's office." Mad Dog had injected a fresh shell into the breach of his shotgun. "Trust me."

I felt that now, after all those assured and overly-confident statements he'd made, was a good time to take Luther Longmire down a notch or two.

"You hear that blast?" I asked. "The one that started the shootout in your building here."

"Why?" His tone had already grown less cocksure.

"In my palm I hold some of that same C-4."

It took a few moments for Luther to configure a response. "Well, you can't use it. You'll kill yourself in the process."

He had a point. And while I didn't want to die, he didn't have to know that. "I'm ready to go, Longmire. You took everything I love. And I hope that asshole cousin of yours in there heard that."

Three hillbillies in overalls edged slowly from behind some crates toward the bottom of the stairs. I went ahead and pasted the explosive to Luther's office door

241

and removed my cell phone, dialing the number Mad Dog had given me. I had my thumb on the send button, my eyes closed. If I was going to go, I was taking Luther and Amara with me.

My eyes closed, all I could hear were their footsteps ascending the stairs. I was moments away from hitting send on the cell when what sounded like twenty guns firing at once pierced my ears and forced me to open my eyes.

Mad Dog and Paul were on either side of the bottom of the stairwell, filling Luther's three henchmen with machine gun fire and buckshot. Falling down the steps, one of the hillbillies got three shots off, all of which hit Paul in the chest. Paul stumbled back against a crate then collapsed. When the gun thug landed on the concrete floor at the bottom of the stairs. Mad Dog dropped his shotgun, drew his revolver, and finished off the guard who'd shot Paul.

"I guess I don't have to go with you," I said to Luther. "As it turns out. I'm off to brighter horizons. You two have a nice last few seconds together."

As I walked down the steps, I heard the door open behind me. Luther appeared from within the office dark and raised his token Magnum. He opened his mouth to say something, probably something he thought was smart, then a rose pedal appeared in the middle of his chest, then another, each wound matched with the sharp crack of gunfire. Luther fell in the doorway, his head hitting the last step before the office.

Amara stepped out from the darkened doorway and looked down at Luther's body, then at me. She was crying, a smoking .38 revolver in her left hand. "He made me do it, Jon. He made me do all of it."

I peered down at Mad Dog who had Paul's arm slung around his shoulder, helping the wounded dope soldier walk. "Do whatever you're gonna do, dipshit," Mad Dog yelled. "But we got product and cash to load, so hurry up."

44

WE LOADED AS many crates of heroin that would fit into the U-Haul Mad Dog had rented that morning. The only cash on the premises was Luther's escape money. Mad Dog determined that thanks to the Kevlar, at worst, our friend had a broken rib or two. I'd disarmed Amara, trusting her about as much as a vampire for a blowjob. But I'd yet to take any punitive actions for her betrayal.

"That was actually smart," Mad Dog said, driving the U-Haul, me riding shotgun. Paul rode in the back, wounded, but alert enough to keep watch over Amara. "She wouldn't have been able to open Luther's safe otherwise."

"She'll turn on us the first chance she has, right?"

Mad Dog took a moment to reply.

We stopped at an abandoned rest stop just north of Lexington where I'd left a used El Camino I'd found on Craigslist. Paul and Amara stepped out of the U-Haul. The four of us were clearly ready to decide where we went from here.

I took out my key ring, removed the one that went to my new junk car and tossed the others to Paul.

"Bookstore's yours," I told him. "Paperwork is on the desk. All you gotta do is sign it and send it to the Secretary of State in Frankfort. Bookstore is yours and so is my part in the game, if you want it that is."

Paul just nodded. I knew he'd have to think about whether he was ready for another go at the drug trade.

"Mad Dog might just help you learn the ropes," I added.

"The man proved himself today." Mad Dog placed his arm around Paul's shoulder, a gesture that surprised us all.

"What are you gonna do?" Mad Dog asked me.

"I'm out," I said. "Which essentially means I gotta stay out of Louisville. For a long time."

"What about her?" Paul asked.

"You guys get in the truck and get on out of here," I said. "I'd like a moment alone with the girl."

After they were gone, Amara started her crying again. The girl should have been an actress. She hadn't been crying when they dragged me off to drop me in the river with a hole in my forehead.

"Stop." I held up my hand. "Just stop."

"What are you going to do with me?" she asked as she wiped away the tears she'd forced.

"You know, Amara, I'd never read to a woman before."

"We'll always have Yeats," she said.

I drew the H-K with the suppressor Mad Dog had handed me when we'd decided what to do about the girl. As usual, she looked lovely. Dressed all in black, like for a funeral after which she'd make love.

"You're right, darling." I shot her twice in the face. "We'll always have Yeats."